"Are yo[...]

"N-no." She gave a tremulous laugh. "This London traffic is a hazardous thing."

He hauled her up higher against him, plopping her down on his lap. Thankfully, it eased the discomfort of her cramped legs as he settled her over him, however much inappropriate.

There was no need for him to hold her like this. Not any longer. There was no need for them to be tangled up like this, however cozy and exciting. And yet she couldn't move . . . and he wasn't lifting herself or himself away.

"I'm fine," she reassured him, releasing an agitated breath and rubbing at the tip of her nose.

Concern was writ all over his face, creasing his brow. Those deep-set eyes of his, so dark and intent, churned her insides. His hands flexed on her arms, and she looked down, noting how very much she was splayed against him, indecently nestled in his lap, her skirts a great pile of muslin around them.

She inhaled, sucking in a great breath, and *that* was a mistake. He smelled so very nice. Like soap and leather and . . . *him*. Even with her hand over her nose, his scent enveloped her.

By Sophie Jordan

Sophie Jordan

THE DUKE EFFECT

❧ The Rogue Files ❧

AVONBOOKS

An Imprint of HarperCollins*Publishers*

THE DUKE EFFECT. Copyright © 2020 by Sharie Kohler. All rights reserved. Printed in the United States of America. No part of this book may be used or reproduced in any manner whatsoever without written permission except in the case of brief quotations embodied in critical articles and reviews. For information, address Harper-Collins Publishers, 195 Broadway, New York, NY 10007.

First Avon Books mass market printing: November 2020

Print Edition ISBN: 978-0-06-288545-6
Digital Edition ISBN: 978-0-06-288540-1

Cover design by Patricia Barrow
Cover illustration by Jon Paul Ferrara
Author photo by Country Park Portraits

Avon, Avon & logo, and Avon Books & logo are registered trademarks of HarperCollins Publishers in the United States of America and other countries.

HarperCollins is a registered trademark of HarperCollins Publishers in the United States of America and other countries.

FIRST EDITION

20 21 22 23 24   QGM   10 9 8 7 6 5 4 3 2 1

For Kim Woodson.
You are missed. Today, tomorrow, always.

THE DUKE EFFECT

The Village Gazette

On Tuesday the 14th inst. expired most regrettably, in this shire of Esswick, the remaining son of the most distinguished Duke and Duchess of Birchwood. Only thirty years of age, the honorable Lord Winston Birchwood died of miasma after suffering from a festering splinter wound.

His disposition was most ebullient, his cheer infectious to all. His lordship will be most sorely missed among family, friends and the residents of Hampleton, home to the most venerable Birchwood seat. May he rest in peace and grace alongside his recently departed brothers, Lord Albert Birchwood and Lord Malcolm Birchwood, who went to their heavenly rewards before him this past February and May, respectively.

Chapter 1

January, 1866
The Bengal Duars

Colonel Constantine Sinclair was not a man given to drink, but were he such an individual, he would be well into his cups by now and on his way to a state of mindlessly deep inebriation.

He carefully set the letter down on the desk before him and leaned back in his chair to stare unseeingly ahead. Dimly he registered the sounds of male conversation and laughter outside his tent. This mingled with the even fainter sounds of the jungle at dusk.

They'd camped here for almost eight months

now. Most of the wildlife kept their distance, but he was ever aware of the fact that it was always there, teeming and nipping at the edges of the camp. Last week a soldier had strayed too far during the night and become lost. They'd only found his remains in the morning. It was a vital reminder to all to remain vigilant.

The world was forever full of wild and irrepressible things, ready to devour you. Whether it be a tiger or a splinter wound. Life offered no assurances. He'd always known that to be the case, but he was starkly reminded of it now.

When the camp fell asleep and the sounds of the men quieted, he would be able to hear the nearby Teesta River. It was the most peaceful part of the day, when the noise went dead and there was calm—or the illusion of it, at any rate.

He oft liked to ride along the river in the early dawn, when the world was waking, with the verdant hills rising up alongside him shrouded in mist. This time of year was pleasant in the Duars, a marked difference to the monsoon season when they had first arrived.

Now he would be leaving all of this . . . but not by his free will.

Duty compelled him home.

Various aromas penetrated the walls of his tent. Food cooking over campfires. He'd already eaten, but his meal sat like a rock in his now-twisting stomach. In the distance a mandolin played. Several voices lifted in song, accompanying the instrument, but it did nothing to ease his spirits.

It was not an unfamiliar scenario, an evening like this. Nor was it even an unfamiliar song. Corporal Jones sang "Fair Rosamond" often. The ballad was a favorite among the men.

What was unfamiliar was the letter he'd just tossed down on his desk from the Duke of Birchwood's steward. A letter summoning him home.

England.

Home.

Birchwood House.

He found himself glaring at the parchment as though he could will it into flame. Into a mound of smoldering ash.

Constantine had not thought of that place as home in a good many years. Home to him had been an army tent for over half his life. *Hellfire.* Even a muddy battlefield felt more like home to him than what he had left behind in England as a green lad. That green lad he had once been was gone.

The flap to his tent parted and his batman entered. "Whew." Morris removed his cap and ran a hand through his hair. "Wind picking up. Storm coming from the east."

A storm was indeed coming.

"Well, I'll be heading decidedly *west* on the morrow."

His batman looked up sharply as he sank down on his cot. "Did you get orders to move us west?"

"In a manner." He glanced at the letter again. "*I* have received orders. You and the men will stay put."

Morris followed his gaze to the rough-hewn desk with a frown. "I don't follow your meaning."

"I've been summoned home, Morris."

"Home as in England?"

Constantine took a moment to react, too preoccupied with digesting this turn in his life. Eventually he nodded while gazing at the letter bearing the distantly familiar ducal seal as though it were a living, breathing thing that might rise up to snap its teeth at him. "The Duke of Birchwood has spoken."

The grand nobleman was still etched solidly in Constantine's memory with his bushy gray muttonchops and wintry blue stare that could cut straight through you. The duke was perhaps the most prominent of his childhood memories, rising above all like a stone edifice. He remembered his parents only vaguely, as snatches of water-colored images flashing through his mind.

They'd sickened from cholera and perished when he was but seven years. After the loss of his mother and father, he'd desperately wanted the love and approval of his father's distant kinsman upon whose doorstep he was deposited.

His father had been a simple solicitor and his mother of even more humble origins—a shop-girl from the East End. Rough beginnings aside, Constantine still remembered the gentle way she would stroke his head and brush back his hair as she sang him to sleep.

He'd been a broken little boy when he'd arrived at the duke's Mayfair mansion. He'd thought it a palace, so grand had it appeared to his young eyes with its countless liveried servants and gleaming fixtures and glorious art and the vaulted ceilings that seemed to touch the sky.

For ten years, the duke scarcely spoke to Constantine, but the man had done well by him. Birchwood had brought him up when his parents died. No one had forced him to do so. He was a duke of the realm and he had taken Constantine in. He'd given him a roof over his head, a chamber of his own, food on his plate and allowed him to be tutored alongside his three sons.

Constantine owed him.

When one considered how perfectly reasonable it would have been to have turned Constantine over to an orphanage or workhouse. Their family connection was, after all, tenuous at best. He'd even purchased Con his commission at the age of seventeen, and no paltry commission either. He'd come into the army as an officer and had reached the rank of colonel by the age of thirty. He liked to think he had moved through the ranks due to his own merit, but his connection to the Duke of Birchwood was mentioned upon his every promotion.

Now, a year later, there had been talk of another promotion. He supposed that was moot now.

"Why have you been summoned home?"

"It seems the duke's son has met with an unfortunate end. He is gone," he said in an even voice that reflected none of his inner turmoil.

"Dead?" Morris asked as though requiring clarification.

"Yes."

He felt a flash of remorse over Winston's passing. As the eldest of his cousins and the one closest in age to Constantine, Winston had set the tone of tolerance toward Constantine, and his younger two cousins followed his lead. Still, he could never claim to have been particularly close

to any of the duke's sons. Cousins four times removed, there had always been a gulf between
them—an awareness that he was naught but
a foundling from the wrong side of the family
tree. They'd never been cruel to him . . . merely
detached. Coolly disinterested. Rather, they had
treated him as a stray cat, largely ignoring him
but occasionally giving him a scratch behind the
ears.

Now with this letter informing him that Winston was dead—appallingly fast on the heels of
Constantine's younger two cousins who had also
expired—he felt only a numb sense of shock and
dismay at what this signified for him.

"I thought the Duke of Birchwood's two sons
already died? You received word of that many
months ago. Why now are you being called—"

"Oh, allow me to clarify. This is a third son,"
he quickly supplied with a shake of his head. He
felt as though he'd taken a thump to the skull. It
was all very bewildering. "Birchwood's eldest and
third son has expired. The three are gone now."

All three.

Gone.

The Duke of Birchwood's three sons were *all*
gone from this earth. Constantine had received
word of Malcolm's and Albert's untimely deaths
not even a year ago, and now Winston was gone.

How did three brothers perish in the span of one year? All from different ailments? What were the odds? Winston from a splinter. Albert from choking on a bit of venison. Malcolm from a broken neck.

The duke now had no heir in which to hand down his title and property, entailed or otherwise—at least to no direct issue of his own. A circumstance that could never have been predicted considering his fruitful union with the duchess.

"Bloody hell," his batman muttered, rubbing a hand over his forehead.

Constantine rose and made his way toward the nearby bottle of brandy. He rarely indulged in spirits. Too often, he'd been roused from bed to attend to one matter or another and he did not wish to be muddleheaded on those occasions. This felt an appropriate exception.

He poured the amber liquid into his glass and downed it in one gulp. "Bloody hell, indeed."

"Who could have imagined such a tragic thing? *All* his sons lost in the span of one year?" Morris's voice faded away.

He'd seen evidence enough of tragedy in his service to the empire. But three coddled, privileged sons of a duke dying in England was wildly irregular.

Constantine turned and faced his batman. The

two had been in service together for over a decade. Con knew he would honorably serve whoever arrived as his successor.

"And yet there we have it," he said. "All are dead," he finished. "And I am now the duke's heir." He took a deep breath. One that felt necessary for lungs that felt suddenly too tight and starving for air. "I'm leaving for England tomorrow," he announced grimly.

He had been summoned. Responsibility demanded he go.

Morris nodded grimly. "Never have I imagined you would leave all this"—he motioned around them—"to become a bloody nob."

Nor would he have envisioned such a fate either. He had thought the military would be the totality of his life. He'd wanted nothing else for himself. "I haven't any choice."

Constantine would do what every soldier did in battle. He'd carry the flag. Pick it up where it had dropped from the hands of the fallen and carry on.

He'd become the duke and take on all the duties that had been meant for the true heir, for the three before him, and continue on.

Because that was what a proper soldier did.

His life would never be his own again.

Chapter 2

There were females in this life who were born to be wives and mothers.

They knew that was their destiny from the moment they could string syllables together to form words. It was etched into their souls. A part of their very composite, scored into their genetic structure. They embraced it.

As girls they played with dolls and toy houses and tiny prams, simulating the scenes of domesticity they witnessed their own mothers and aunts and neighbors playing out. Eleanora Langley knew those girls well. Her sisters had been those girls playing at being mothers and wives. Now they were in reality mothers and wives.

Nora supposed it was the natural order of

things. Except she had never been one to fall into the natural order of things.

As a child, Nora had mimicked Papa and pretended to be a physician, caring for her sick dolls and stuffed animals' broken bones. That definitely set her apart from her sisters and other girls.

And now such playacting had turned into reality. Her sisters were, in fact, wives and mothers (or soon to be mothers) whilst she was not. She cared for the sick and set broken bones on actual people rather than dolls and stuffed animals now.

Such a vocation definitely separated Nora from the masses.

Unlike the other females in the village, she was the first one free of the family pew and out of the church doors. She was not keen on lingering to socialize with myriad neighbors and friends. There'd been enough forced socialization and threat of fire and brimstone from the vicar for the day. Enough until next Sunday when she would once again be stuck in the family pew.

She strode quickly ahead. Stepping out into the churchyard, she lifted her face to the morning sun and inhaled a contented breath. Immediately, she began searching for her family's liveried carriage, eager to depart for home. She'd done her duty for the day. She was ready to take her leave and return home. She had many tasks waiting her attention and she was eager to get back to them.

She tugged on her gloves and squinted up at the sun fighting to break through the ever-clinging clouds. At least it was not raining. This spring had been a torrential downpour and she was ready for the days of summer where she might explore the countryside once again for herbs.

She glanced behind her, hoping that her sisters were quick on her heels. A vain wish, indeed. They just cleared the doors and emerged outside when they were intercepted by the Harken-Dales. She sighed. Of course.

Her brothers-in-law were equally popular. Gentlemen converged on them, too. Such pandering could take all afternoon.

Nora shifted on her feet. She was not quite so popular, which was not anything particularly new or particularly wounding to her ego.

Popularity was not anything for which she had ever aspired. Balls, teas, parties were all fine and well, but she would rather be working in her laboratory or toiling in her herb garden or attending to a patient.

Her sisters were married. That, she had learned,

raised women in the world's estimation—
specifically in the estimation of the villagers of
Brambledon. Unfair as that may be, it was the
reality of things.

Charlotte, historically the most reticent of the
Langley sisters, was by far the *most* popular. A
strange turn of events, indeed. Of course the
reason for her sudden popularity was easy to
understand. The cause happened to be the cute-
as-a-bunny ten-month-old baby in her arms.
Motherhood, apparently, was another cause for
popularity.

In fact, motherhood, perhaps, topped wife-
hood. While her sisters' marriages had lifted
them in the world's estimation . . . motherhood
had lifted them to exalted status.

A glance over her shoulder revealed Mrs.
Harken-Dale cooing over Charlotte's baby. A line
was fast gathering behind her.

"Gah." Nora expelled a heavy breath. "We're
going to be here forever."

She admired her niece as much as the next person. More so. They were kin, after all. But she did
not relish having to wait whilst everyone gushed
over little Cordelia.

Nora's gaze skittered to her eldest sister. Marian was increasing now, and everyone gushed

over her nearly as much as Charlotte and little Cordelia.

As her sisters were rushed by the matrons of the village, Nora walked briskly toward the Warrington carriage. She would wait inside. Perhaps that would encourage them to say their farewells and break away.

No one attempted to intercept her. Unless someone had a boil that required lancing, Nora was not in demand.

A liveried groom lowered the step and moved to open the door for her. She reached for his extended hand, ready to ascend and wait inside.

"Thank you, Thomas," she murmured, nestling her fingers in his palm.

Once she was settled on the squabs, she sat and waited, willing herself to patience.

Of course, patience was not her strong suit. It never had been. In her restlessness, she slipped off her gloves and idly ran her fingers over the calluses marring her palms.

"Oh, bother." Without hailing the groom for assistance, she took flight out the door not facing the church. She cast a glance back. Thomas stared after her from his perch, looking quite puzzled.

She waved a hand in the air. "The day is so lovely. Tell my sisters I will walk home."

She marched forward, unaware if he called a reply and uncaring if he did. She was accustomed to going about her own pursuits in the manner she chose. Her sisters were accustomed as well, and would feel no surprise to find her gone.

Contentment suffused her as she strolled through the countryside at an easy pace, leaving the bustling churchyard and village behind and enjoying the fine weather. Buds poked from several trees and shrubs, heralding the onset of spring. It was an excellent day for gathering herbs if only she had brought her satchel along with her. Instantly she decided she would hasten to her chamber, change her garments and gather the things she required for collecting herbs.

When she arrived at Haverston Hall it was to find Marian and her husband not yet returned. Goodness, if Nora hadn't slipped away she would still be stuck there.

Shaking her head, she dashed up to her chamber and made quick work of shedding her garments, twisting about and doing her best to undo the buttons at her back without tearing them loose. Many a button had flown on occasions before, scattered to the corners of her chamber.

She knew the maid assigned to her upon moving into Haverston Hall rued the day she had landed Nora as a charge. Nora was forever uncooperative, avoiding custom and dressing herself, undressing herself, doing her own hair, tending her fire and pulling down her own bed at night. She was every lady's maid's nightmare, but Bea's especially. Bea had said as much.

Considering the manner of activity she had planned for the rest of the day, she donned one of her old costumes. A simple gray blouse and skirt with an embroidered belt. She had worn the attire often before Marian married the duke—when Nora was naught but a simple country maid.

Life had been hard then, with little money and debtors hunting them and a belly that was never quite full. Fear for their future was a very real thing.

Now there was no fear. And yet life had been simpler then. Simpler when she'd had nothing. No money. No prospects, certainly.

Now there were expectations, as much as she disliked those expectations and chafed beneath the weight of them.

She descended the stairs and made her way free of the house without encountering anyone. She exhaled. It always felt a little easier to breathe when she was clear of Haverston Hall.

She basked in the fine day, her long strides quickly covering the distance, soon depositing her at her destination on the far side of the estate.

The secluded little lagoon was a place she had occasionally visited, swimming in the waters as a child, although she supposed she had been trespassing in those days.

She rounded the pond where several white willows crowded the water's edge, shielding a good portion of the water from the sun. Nora was well familiar with these particular willows. She'd harvested willow bark from them regularly every spring, even before Warrington had taken residence at Haverston Hall . . . before he met and subsequently married Marian.

Papa had been the one to show her how such a thing was done . . . and where all the willows were to be found in the shire. At least in so far as he knew. The closest willow tree to her house no longer thrived. Papa had foraged from it every spring until it had finally died.

She'd been delighted when she one day looked up during her swim to notice the trio of willow trees. She had at once set about harvesting the bark, but judiciously. She had no wish for the trees to perish for the sake of medicine. What good would it do anyone if she harvested the bark too aggressively and destroyed the trees?

And of course, there was her work.

Willow bark was a common ingredient for many of her experimental tonics. She was constantly researching ways in which to improve the suffering among the injured and ill. It had been an area of particular interest for her father, and she had taken up the banner.

She winced as she considered the tonic she had made for Charlotte. She had thought it quite harmless. Willow bark had been among its components. All the ingredients she had used before. Some together. Some apart. And yet nothing strange or new. She only altered the levels from previous variations.

And yet how that tonic had dramatically altered the course of Charlotte's life.

Historically, her sister suffered from terrible cramping in the days preceding her menses. Nora felt as though she were close to a breakthrough when she delivered a new mixture to her sister, hopeful that this particular concoction might mitigate her pains. Nora had in no way anticipated the most incredible outcome.

She winced again. Nora did indeed reduce her sister's cramping, but she also created a host of other symptoms for which she could not have accounted. She might approach life with a clinical eye and have a strong grasp of the workings of the human body, but she was still a maid. She had never given a great deal of thought to matters such as arousal.

Never had she considered lust to be such an altering and powerful condition, where an individual's physical state could outweigh her mental faculties, but that is precisely what had happened to Charlotte when she took Nora's tonic.

Nora had invented an aphrodisiac.

Incredible as such a thing sounded, it was true. Nora had catapulted her shy, reticent sister into the throes of desire. Thankfully, such a circumstance had not resulted in anything dire. Quite the opposite.

When Nora considered the situation, she could only feel inordinately pleased with herself. Because of her tonic, Charlotte was blissfully in love and happily married and mother to a healthy child. Perhaps it was bigheaded of her, but she could not help herself. Wrong or right, she was proud of herself—or rather, proud of her tonic. Even if she didn't know what to do with it now. She couldn't very well go about dosing people with an aphrodisiac, after all.

Still, her talents had never brought about such marvelous results before. As far as she knew she had helped people through their ailments, but saved no lives. It made her feel warm inside to know she had played a role in bringing about Charlotte and Kingston's happy union . . . and the life of her niece. She felt giddy at the knowledge.

Nora stood back and carefully evaluated the three trees, noting the areas where she had harvested bark before. Biting her lip, she worried the tender flesh just as she worried over permanently damaging the trees. Papa had warned her against foraging too forcefully. She could cripple the tree and that would not be the thing at all.

She continued to appraise the three trees, marking the lighter skinned patches where bark had been removed from the trunks in previous years. "Well," she announced to herself. She was guilty of talking to herself whilst she worked. "It must be done." But done right.

The only right way was to climb high up the tree to collect bark off some of the upper branches that had been spared of earlier foraging. It was much wiser to cut bark from one of the branches rather than the trunk.

She adjusted the strap of her satchel across her chest and hiked up her skirts, tucking the front hem into the belt at her waist. Thankfully, she'd spent a girlhood climbing trees all over the shire. Even though it had been some time since she had done so, it felt a familiar task.

She searched and found a handhold and hefted herself up, her boots slipping and scuffling until they gained a foothold. Grunting, she scaled the trunk until she reached the first outcropping of branches, wishing she had worn her gloves. Her palms were stinging.

She steadied her weight, wedging her boots in the V of branches. She purposefully did not look down. Not that she was scared of heights. It just seemed sensible to avoid doing so. Intent on her task, she crawled out onto one of the sturdier branches. Carefully balancing her weight, she squeezed her thighs around the branch and inched out as far as she dared, determined to collect bark far from areas she had already harvested.

Pausing, she fumbled inside her satchel for her small paring knife.

It was precarious business. She moved cautiously, slowly, so as not to lose her balance. Soon, she was slicing slivers of thumb-size bark, tucking them inside her palm until she had well over a dozen pieces.

Once again, she fumbled inside her satchel, retrieving the small jar within and securing the slivers inside the vessel, screwing the lid back on tightly once she was finished.

"There," she breathed heavily, satisfied with her efforts. It should result in a fine amount of willow bark tea . . . with quite a bit left over for her to experiment with in her various tinctures and tonics.

A flash of movement below caught her gaze and she froze, her eyes flaring wide in her face. She gasped.

There was a person. A *man*.

A man directly beneath her in the water.

She recoiled at the unexpected sight of him. *There was a strange man in her pond! How dare he!*

The motion upset her balance. There was no swallowing her cry as she wobbled upon her perch, attempting to regain her balance to no avail. Her clenched knees lost their grip.

She slipped, tilting sideways, and then went down . . . falling. Dropping with an unceremonious graceless splash in the pond.

Chapter 3

*N*ora emerged, sputtering and squawking before the very individual to have caught her so unawares. The *wretched* individual who had no right to be in the Warrington pond. Who was this interloper?

She shoved the wet, heavy skeins of her hair back from her face and gawked at him. He stared at her with equal astonishment from eyes the color of coal. His wet hair was equally dark and plastered about his head in wild disarray.

"What are you doing here?" she demanded, treading water and not with much ease as her skirts had come untucked and were a dire nuisance, tangling amid her kicking legs.

He looked from her and up to the tree, deduc-

ing her origin and doubtlessly confirming she
had not fallen from the sky.

"Did you not hear my question?" she demanded. Water splashed against her chin and
lips as she bobbed in the water, and she coughed
a bit.

"I'm availing myself of a swim in this pond,"
the stranger finally and very reasonably replied.

Far too reasonably. As though trespassing were
a reasonable and acceptable thing. As though
availing himself of someone's pond for a swim
were a reasonable thing to do and not at all il-
licit act.

Certainly, she had done the same thing for
years, but that was neither here nor there.

"I can clearly see that. It's your presumption to
indulge in a swim *here* that I find so very objectionable, sirrah."

Sirrah?

Did that come from her lips? She sounded such
a prig. As dour and grating as Mrs. Pembroke
from the village. Nora had been forced into that
unpleasant woman's company on far too many
occasions. She could scarcely stomach the lady . . .
and she certainly could not stomach the notion
that she was anything like the wretched woman.

"You're trespassing." She winced at the shrill
edge to her voice.

Instead of answering that charge, he replied with equanimity, "What were you doing up in that tree?"

"Never you mind my business," she sputtered. Why was he *still* here in this pond? With her? "Get out! Out!"

He lifted a hand and wiped it over his face as though clearing it of water droplets would also help to clear away the vision of her before him. Of course it was for naught, she was still very much before him. No magical creature but flesh and blood.

His lashes were long and dark, jagged wet spikes that snared her attention—even given her state of distress. The small detail should be beneath her notice. Such things usually were. She rarely gave much consideration to the male gender as a whole unless the man was a patient in need of treatment. Certainly a man's lashes had never caught her interest before.

This man, she noted, had likely never been ill a day in his life. He appeared quite robust. The very vision of health. He appeared to have no trouble treading water. Water lapped at his rather large and well-formed shoulders.

"Getting out of this pond presents some difficulty," he finally answered.

"How is that?" she asked, snapping her focus away from his bare shoulders.

"You see"—he glanced toward the shore—"my clothes are over there."

She followed his gaze, her stare arresting on the pile of clothing on the pebbled ground. She gave a croak and swung her attention back on him.

Evidently his shoulders weren't the only part of him that happened to be bare. He was fully *un*clothed and only inches from her. Thankfully, she could not see the rest of him through the murky depths of the pond—not that she attempted to gain a glimpse.

He looked at her rather expectantly. He clearly anticipated for her to turn into a blushing and squeamish female, exclaiming in maidenly protest.

She lifted her chin in an attempt at dignity. He would be sadly disappointed over her lack of histrionics. She had never been a female given to maidenly airs. Another thing that set her apart from other ladies.

"I can assure you, sir . . . you are not in possession of anything I have not seen before."

Astonishment flickered in his dark eyes . . . and something else. *Interest* perhaps? For a moment the sentiment was there and then it vanished.

"Indeed," he murmured slowly, as though digesting her bold claim.

She gave a hard nod. "Indeed."

"Well," he said, his deep voice rumbling between them with an austerity that even her dukely brother-in-law failed to manage. "If you have no objections then."

Turning, he headed for the shore, gliding smoothly, offering her a glimpse of his muscled male back, youthful and strong, undulating with his movements. An inconvenient lump formed in her throat. *Who knew a man's back could be so riveting?*

The surface of the pond hardly even rippled as he swam away, which seemed a testament to his inherent agility. She did not have a great deal of exposure to agile men. Most were patients who were aging or ill. Except for her brothers-in-law, of course. But she did not see them as men. They were married to her sisters. They existed in a category of their own.

If you have no objections . . .

Oh, she *objected*. Heartily so.

Inside she was raging at this man's intrusion on her pond, and upon her peace . . . and his disruption to her equilibrium.

She watched, frozen in the middle of the pond—except for her treading legs, which kept her from sinking. Although drowning didn't sound too terrible right now because her face burned hot with mortification. She'd never been one to ogle a man, but here she was doing that very thing. It irked her. She had always thought herself immune to such behavior, but there was no stopping her gasp as he emerged from the pond, revealing himself inch by inch, water sluicing down the long lines of his big body.

All of his body. From the back, at any rate.

His broad shoulders tapered to a narrow waist and hips. But it was his backside that most captured her attention. The tight, well-formed cheeks of his derriere. Saliva pooled in her mouth. A curious impulse seized her to squeeze those cheeks . . . give them a swat and see if they were as firm as they looked.

Madness. She wasn't a licentious person. She attributed the urge to her scientific nature. She was a *curious* person. Nothing more.

He bent and gathered up his garments. Turning, he faced her and she saw that his stomach was flat, his chest lightly sprinkled with hair, the sinews of his torso rippling with his movements beneath taut skin.

For all his great height and breadth of shoulders, he was lean and rangy and could use a few additional meals. And yet his strength and power felt palpable. She sensed it in the same way the air felt charged preceding a storm.

Again, this was merely her professional opinion and not that of a female given to appreciating the male form in any carnal manner.

A familiar quote from *Julius Caesar* sprang to mind . . . *a lean and hungry look; He thinks too much; such men are dangerous.*

Treading water, she swallowed against the thickness in her throat.

"I'll leave you to your pond, miss." He executed a bow. Rather ridiculous under the circumstances, but there was nothing ridiculous about this man. Indeed not. As he bent at the waist with his clothes bunched up in front of him to shield his manhood from her eyes, she could only squint, peering at him as though she might see through the garments. Impossible, of course. Unfortunate, that.

Unfortunate?

What was wrong with her? Clearly her scientific curiosity was getting the best of her and edging into new territory. *Sexual* curiosity.

Was it any wonder? Her sisters were constantly exchanging heated glances with their husbands, touching and brushing against each other in small ways they thought to be discreet.

She swam carefully for the shoreline, reminding herself that she did not know this man. She picked a spot to emerge a safe distance from him. Water rushed from her body, dripping down her heavily sodden garments as she rose from the pond, eyeing him warily. "I was not here to swim," she grumbled.

"But this is your pond upon which I trespass?"

She hesitated before giving a brief nod of assent. It was her brother-in-law's pond, but she would not go into that with this stranger.

"Well then. As requested, your privacy." He gestured around them. "Feel free to continue falling from trees."

She snorted. Falling from trees, indeed? Did he think she fell into the pond on purpose? It really was quite lowering. She was more skilled than that. His presence was to blame for her lapse in physical adroitness. He had startled her.

Before she could correct him of his misapprehension, however, he was gone.

With a swift turn, he disappeared into the foliage. A horse soon nickered from inside the thicket. He was not on foot then. That meant he was taking himself off with all swiftness. Good riddance.

Confident she was again alone, she turned her attention to her satchel still hanging from her person, and quickly inspected the jar inside. A relieved breath escaped her. The slivers of bark were still safely inside. The lid had held fast and that troubling man was gone. All good things. She had her equilibrium back. She had enough work to occupy her without adding matters of erotic curiosity to her plate. She'd leave that for others who were searching for a man to bring them fulfillment.

Nora was no such female.

Tucking the jar back inside her satchel, she gave it a satisfied pat and headed in the direction of Haverston Hall, cringing at the sensation of her heavy, wet garments clinging to her body. At least it was not a cold day. It would have been even more miserable if she had fallen into the pond during the winter. Of course, *he* would not have been indulging in a swim in the midst of winter. There would have been that benefit.

She walked, water squishing from her boots. Not a comfortable sensation.

No doubt she would have to explain to Mrs. Conally what happened. The housekeeper would take one look at her and demand an explanation. She was not easily put off with excuses or tactics of avoidance.

She knew better than to enter through the grand front doors of the house where her arrival would be much noticed and exclaimed over. The staff was on high alert these days when it came to her. Her sisters had conspired to make certain she now took her meals with the family, forbidding her from asking for a tray in her room where she could eat as she worked. Alone.

It was this very aloneness they so objected to. She didn't know why they should disapprove. It did not bother Nora. Marian and Charlotte insisted she was on her way to becoming a hermit. A terrible fate, apparently, and one they refused to allow her. What they failed to understand was that she was the happiest when she was buried in her work. It's what she loved.

She slipped through the servants' entrance in the back of the hall, listening for a moment, dripping in the corridor, to the sounds of the staff busy in the kitchen. They would be readying for luncheon. If her sister and the duke were not yet home, they would be soon.

It was now or never whilst the servants were so occupied and below stairs in the kitchen. She darted up the stairs and slipped inside her room undetected, setting her satchel down carefully on her work table.

She stripped off her clothes, letting the sodden garments drop heavily. Unpinning her hair, she worked a brush through the half-dry mass of snarled waves. It really was an inconvenience and such a bother. She should cut it.

She selected a fresh dress and donned it. This frock was just as plain and modest as the last one she wore. It was another one from the old days. The days before Warrington and her life at Haverston Hall. There had been no fine dresses in her life then. It made no sense to wear one of her new elegant gowns when she was working in her laboratory. In truth, she had little use for the gowns, but they were what was expected of a duke's sister-in-law, even an unorthodox duke like Warrington who eschewed life in Town and could scarcely be prevailed upon to rub elbows with his peers.

The cotton dress fit her snugly, but the fabric was well-worn and comfortable, even if it did hug her chest too tightly and stretch at the seams in several places, namely her generous hips—they were a definite tribute to the splendid bisques and soufflés Cook was fond of preparing. One welcome perk of her sister marrying a duke; his kitchens were far superior to what she was accustomed.

Just then the door to her chamber opened and Bea entered as Nora managed to do the last button.

"Now Bea," she began, prepared for the dress-

ing down she was certain to receive for not ringing Bea to come and help her. "It was a simple
change of wardrobe that I could do perfectly well
on my own—"

"You've a caller," the maid interrupted. "Ack!
And look at your hair. 'Tis not fit to feed the pigs."
Bea pushed her to sit down before the dressing
table.

"A caller?" Nora frowned at her reflection.
"Who is it?"

Bea focused on her hair with single-minded
zeal. "I do not know. Mrs. Conally told me to
fetch you."

"I am certain it's someone from the village in
need of a poultice or some such." She attempted
to rise.

Bea settled her hands on her shoulders and
pushed her back down. "You'll not be running
downstairs with your hair a tumble. Such a dis-
grace." She tsked her tongue. "It will be a poor
reflection on me and we can't have that."

"Very well," she grumbled, watching as Bea
deftly arranged her hair into plaits and then
pinned them atop her head in a very stylish
fashion.

"There you are." She lightly patted Nora's
head. "Splendid. Very tidy. You should let me attend you every morning."

"Let us not go so far as that," she said as she surged from the chair, glad to be free of Bea's ministrations.

She was no fine lady and would never grow accustomed to all the trappings that went along with being one. She'd grown up in a modest household, with only two servants to wait on their family of six. After Mama and Papa died, after she and her siblings were truly orphaned, they had lost even that. They had to let their beloved staff go.

They had lost so much really and had been left on their own to endure considerable hardships. Nora was accustomed to doing for herself and that would never change.

No matter her shift in fortune, she was an independent woman.

She hastened down the steps, ignoring her growling stomach. That combined with the delicious smells of their impending luncheon drifting from the kitchen reminded her that she'd had no more than a few bites of toast hours ago. The fault was hers. She'd been in such haste, late as usual to breakfast because she'd lost track of time studying a new botanical text that arrived from London. She could scarcely tear herself away from its pages and was eager to return to it.

She spotted Mrs. Conally in the corridor as she came down.

"Oh, there you are, Miss Langley. Your guest awaits you in the drawing room. I've sent in Cate with some tea."

Hopefully scones, too.

"Thank you, Mrs. Conally."

The double doors were parted, awaiting her entrance. She imagined the guest must be of some import if Mrs. Conally secured him (or her) in the drawing room with tea.

She entered the room, noting the gentleman standing at the window. Nora did not recognize him from her vantage. He stood with his back to her, a straight and stalwart figure looking out the mullioned glass at the expansive green lawn. The sunlight struck his hair and it glinted blue-black in the brightness.

His hands were clasped very correctly behind him. That, combined with his erect bearing, gave an impression of severity. It was hard to fathom he might be here due to some sort of ailment. Even without seeing his face he struck her as hale.

She cleared her throat. "Hello, there," she greeted, expecting to recognize him once he turned to face her. If he was here to see her, she had likely met him before. There were few people in Brambledon whom she did not know or whom she had not treated.

He turned and she was not wrong, unfortunately.

She knew him . . . in a manner.

She had seen him before. *Blast it all.* She suspected that when she closed her eyes, she would see him for days to come.

Chapter 4

*N*ora recognized him even though he was respectably clothed this time.

Her last sight of him had been at the pond . . . and he had been naked. She could envision him as she had last observed him, the lines and angles and hollows of his body dappled in sunlight, speckled with droplets of water. He might be standing in an elegant drawing room, but she could strip away his garments in her mind and see him so clearly. *Drat*. She had thought she'd seen the last of him.

"You," she breathed.

"You," he returned, looking mildly jarred at the unexpected sight of her, which echoed their first encounter.

As he looked her up and down, she sensed his judgment and resisted the urge to fidget. Given her attire, he likely thought her a servant. She certainly did not appear to belong in these refined surroundings. He doubtlessly did not think her a member of Warrington's family.

She squared her shoulders and reminded herself that she might not be a highborn lady who presided over drawing rooms, but she resided in this house. She was a member of Warrington's family and she belonged here, however unnatural it felt at times.

She belonged here, and he did not.

Chin aloft, she turned to the footman who stood nearby, tucked into a corner of the room. She'd almost forgotten his presence. The number of servants Warrington kept on staff still astounded her.

"Thank you, Archie. You may leave us."

Ever proper, the footman inclined his head and departed the room.

Once confident he was out of earshot—it would not do for the servants to gossip about her below stairs—she charged ahead. "You've a great deal of cheek calling here, sirrah."

What is he doing here? Is he here to apologize to the master of the house for availing himself of his pond?

"Have I?" he asked, bowing slightly, as though

in afterthought, but his gaze remained fastened on her as he extended her the courtesy.

She did not like that stare on her one little bit.

That dark gaze of his was unnerving. His eyes were so dark it was impossible to determine where his pupils ended and began. Much too unnerving and much too unreadable. She felt exposed. As though he were peeling back all her layers to see to the core of her, which was as impossible as it was ridiculous.

This man, this stranger, did not know her . . . and he could not see to the truth of her.

So few people could. Her friends from girlhood had all grown up and married and started their families. They were busy with their own households and did not have time for her—unless it was for medicinal reasons. Sometimes she wondered if even her sisters truly understood her. They were happily married, and were often pointing out gentlemen in the village to her, bachelors they deemed suitable . . . as though they believed Nora should join their ranks and marry, too. As though it were that easy to fall in love. As though Nora even wanted to.

"Indeed. Have you come here to apologize for earlier today?" she repeated.

"Apologize?" He said the word slowly, as though it were a foreign thing he was testing out on his tongue. "No. No, I did not come here to apologize."

"You did not?" She canted her head and sharpened her gaze on him. Everything about his presence here baffled her and an uneasy sensation started in her belly. "What then are you doing here, sir?"

"I've business here, and as for my swim in the pond . . . I merely wished to refresh after my long ride and make myself presentable."

"Hmph." She crossed her arms over her chest. "You've business with Warrington then?"

"I did not say that," he replied rather vaguely. "It was not he with whom I've requested an audience."

They had fetched Nora to attend him. That was true.

Presumably then, he had asked for Nora. She frowned. That made no sense.

"If you're not here for Warrington . . . who then are you here to see?"

"Why, Dr. Langley."

She flinched.

It was strange to hear her father's name uttered in a manner that implied he still lived, that he still walked among them. It had been years since his passing and his absence had faded to a dull ache, but hearing his name spoken out loud by this man was jarring. The dull ache of his loss flared anew to a stinging pain.

"Dr. Langley," she echoed at a whisper.

"Yes, I said as much to the housekeeper."

She nodded, contemplating that. Of course. Mrs. Conally would have sent Nora to answer such a caller rather than make the explanations herself. It was not her place to inform a seemingly well-bred stranger that Dr. Langley was no longer of this earth. Such a task would fall to one of his family members, and Nora was the only one at home presently.

Or perhaps Mrs. Conally even thought their guest meant *Nora* when he asked to see Dr. Langley. Nora did attend to many of the locals, after all, serving their medical needs. No physician had replaced Papa in the community. There was no doctor in Brambledon. Only Nora. She had jokingly been called *doctor* on more than one occasion.

"You've come here to see Dr. Langley," she murmured, seeking clarification, but also, perhaps, stalling. Her mind raced as she contemplated how best to proceed in this situation.

He was beginning to look a fraction exasperated. "Yes, is he not in residence?"

"Ah, he is not . . ."

Why was this so dreadfully awkward?

She was not one to usually stumble over her words. Rather, she often spit them out like torrents of mortar without forethought.

In this moment, however, she was discomfited and at a loss for words.

"When might I return to see him?" he pressed.

"You may not . . ." she murmured.

"Now see here." He was fully exasperated now, a dull flush of color creeping over his cheeks. "I realize we got off to a bad start, but that is no reason to deny me audience with—"

"He is dead, sir." At last. She'd said it. Baldly declared it to a man whose name she still did not know as there had been no proper introductions. Charlotte would be appalled at her lack of gentility. She was always telling Nora she needed to be more mannerly.

Except *proper* could not be applied to any moment of their interactions thus far, so why should Nora now care how bluntly she revealed the news of her father's death?

She must have shocked him. He stared at her for long moments without response.

He blinked a few times and, after some moments, cleared his throat. "I—I am so very sorry to hear that. I was unaware, of course."

She nodded stiffly. "How is it you knew . . . Dr. Langley?"

She believed she would have remembered this man if he'd ever come to Brambledon, but Papa could have met him when he attended one of his conferences in London or Edinburgh.

"I . . . We have never met, that is not in person, but we have corresponded for years."

"I see," she managed to get out.

Corresponded for years . . .

The words sent a chill through her. She squashed the unwelcome sensation. No one would attempt to track Papa down here. She had been writing on his behalf for years now, dispensing medical advice and then signing (er, forging) his name to those missives. It was subterfuge, true, but she did not see the harm in it. She wasn't hurting anyone. Quite the opposite. The people who wrote to Papa wanted help and she possessed the knowledge to assist them. Papa had trained her himself, after all.

The individuals she corresponded with never lived close to Brambledon. She made certain these were not people she would bump into out and about in Society. Some of them were military men who lived on distant shores and were seeking medical advice for their fellow soldiers and those serving under them. Living abroad and, of course, fighting abroad, these soldiers fell prey to uncommon injuries and ailments, and Papa's reputation in the field of pain mitigation was far-reaching.

He shook his head and glanced to the window, looking much troubled. He swung those dark eyes back on her. "When did the doctor . . . er, pass away?"

"Ah, it's been five years now."

"Five years?" He frowned. "You are certain of that?"

She huffed an indignant breath. "I am quite certain of the date of my father's passing."

He blinked. "You are his daughter then?"

She pulled her shoulders back. "I am."

He hesitated, looking her over, and she felt a fresh wave of self-consciousness at her very drab frock.

"Well, daughter or no, you must be mistaken."

She gave a snort and propped her hands on her hips. "Oh, must I be?"

"Indeed, you *must* be. You *are* mistaken." He reached inside his waistcoat and fumbled a bit before brandishing an envelope. "As I have been writing to the good doctor for the last several years. I have here his last letter to me . . . postmarked this very year."

She gaped at the envelope, narrowing her gaze on the neatly penned scrawl on the outside.

The letter was very familiar. Because it was

her letter. She had penned it and she had sent it to him.

Squinting, she made out the name of the recipient. Instantly, her gaze shot back to his face.

No. It could not be. *He* could not be here. *He* could not be *him*.

He was much too . . . young. He was supposed to be a much older man. Not this young. Not this virile . . . not this *this* standing before her.

Clearly, she had grossly miscalculated. She had thought avoiding anyone who lived in proximity to Brambledon would keep her safe from discovery. She had not counted on anyone traveling a great distance, let alone across an ocean, to see her father.

Because that meant only one thing.

This man was here in the flesh to catch her in her deceit.

Chapter 5

*D*r. Langley was dead.

The knowledge rolled through him, obliterating everything in its path, taking with it the last of his hope. It was a blow. A crushing disappointment.

What now?

Upon his return to England, he'd dutifully claimed his new role as heir to the Duke of Birchwood. He'd moved into the London Mayfair residence with the duke and duchess and for the last two months he'd begun learning his new position and what was expected of him.

The duke and duchess were welcoming if not precisely warm. But then they had never been warm people. They were august members of the noblesse. Warmth was not a quality to be found among their ilk. *Your ilk now.*

They'd aged since he'd last seen them. Naturally. But it was not merely the accumulation of years. They wore their grief like a heavy mantle. They'd lost three sons. The toll was profound. Constantine had vowed to do everything he could to ease their grief and lighten their burdens.

The venerable duke wanted to groom him and apprise him of his myriad duties? Very well. Con would allow him that. He would not be known as the Duke of Birchwood who failed and sank the dukedom to ruin. He'd become a sponge and soak up everything the old duke could teach him and honor all those who had come before him.

The duke and duchess wanted him to pay court to his late cousin's betrothed? Very well. He'd pay court to the fine Lady Elise. He'd even propose once a respectable amount of time had passed, assuming the lady was receptive to such an offer from him and didn't view him as second best and inferior to her first choice duke.

He'd never imagined himself married. *Hellfire.* He had thought to make a lifelong career out of the army—and no. He had never planned to be one of those officers who married and took their wives with them on their posts.

The duchess's chronic pain? He'd determined

to tackle that, too. Somehow he would find a way to alleviate her considerable discomfort. The poor woman had suffered enough. If anything happened to her, it would finish the duke. The couple appeared sincerely devoted to each other—a definite anomaly among the aristocracy.

They'd lost their sons, and Constantine was duty bound to care for them now as the heir.

The heir.

It still left his stomach in knots. He'd never wanted the title. Never even thought it possible to possess it—never once had it passed through his consciousness—but it was his now. The responsibility weighed heavily on him—a yoke about his neck from which he would never be free.

When it came to relieving the duchess of her malaise, he'd known instantly the man to see. There was only one person who could help the duchess. Dr. Langley, the man he'd corresponded with for years whilst abroad. Pain alleviation was his specialty. Or rather, it *had* been. Because the man was apparently dead now.

The knots in his stomach squeezed tighter.

The good doctor been dead for some time, which didn't make sense. Not one little bit.

Con had first heard of Langley when he read an article on pain mitigation in a medical journal. He'd found the topic fascinating so he had written to the author: a Dr. Langley of Brambledon, England. That one letter had spawned a long-standing communication. A fascinating string of communication, mostly discussing matters of medicine and treatment for the ill or injured.

Strange as it seemed, he had come to look forward to those letters, appreciating the man's wit and anecdotes. He'd even referred others with medical concerns to Dr. Langley . . . to a dead man, evidently, as he had been deceased for the last five years.

"How is it the man is dead, but I have been communicating with him long after his death? Am I to believe I have been corresponding with a ghost?"

The girl winced and stared at him in mute misery. Her fire was gone. The fire he had witnessed burning so brightly at the pond—*in* the pond—was gone. Her color ran high then, her cheeks bright as apples, doubtlessly fed by her outrage. Although he did not think her temper alone had caused her flushed cheeks.

He suspected she was the sort of female who eschewed bonnets when she traipsed about the countryside. Bold lasses who climbed trees for no explainable reason and dropped into ponds undoubtedly spent a great deal of time traipsing and exposing their faces to the reticent English sun.

Presently, regret was writ all over her expressive face. It was extraordinary, really. He doubted there was ever an emotion she did not flaunt; hot words she did not bite back, an impulse she did not reject. Unlike himself.

All his life he had kept everything carefully tucked away. Emotion was not to be displayed. Reserve was the order of his life, taught to him first living with the Birchwoods, and then in the army.

Her sudden pallor mystified him. "Do my questions distress you?" he asked at her continued silence.

She moistened her lips. "I—"

The drawing room doors opened then. A well-heeled gentleman and lady entered the room arm in arm, both looking mildly intrigued as they glanced back and forth between Constantine and the girl.

He instantly knew the girl was related to the lady. They both possessed the same fine eyes and fair hair. The girl, however, was younger . . . shorter and curvier. She would fill a man's hands.

As soon as the thought entered his mind, he cast it out. However beguiling her curves, she'd already proven herself a termagant and not at all to his tastes.

He preferred more mature women, sophisticated ladies prepared to enter into mutually satisfying liaisons devoid of unnecessary emotion. Women capable of conducting an affair in a dignified manner.

He did not believe in doing anything rashly, which made his sudden departure from Town and his sudden arrival here all the more uncharacteristic of him.

A couple years past, the good doctor had written to him informing him of his change of address. The man had not given any explanation and Con had not inquired. He'd thought perhaps he'd gone to live with a relation at this Haverston Hall. The doctor, he had assumed, was not a young man, after all.

Upon arriving in Brambledon, he'd learned that Haverston Hall was the home of the Duke of Warrington. A curious thing, but he had not let that give him pause. He had stopped at the pond to freshen up. He was covered in dust. He'd eschewed the train and ridden hard from London, after all. As he was here to ask a favor of Dr. Langley, he wanted to present himself well.

He'd toyed with the idea of writing a letter first, but thought it would be more compelling to present his case in person. He had also assumed, likely erroneously, that he would be more difficult to decline in person.

Perhaps Constantine would have his answers at last.

He eyed the formidable-looking gentleman and assumed him to be the Duke of Warrington who reigned over Haverston Hall. He had that air of nobility about him.

"Nora?" the lovely woman inquired. The fact that she was increasing with child did not distract from her beauty or grace. "Who is your guest?"

So the girl was named Nora—and apparently of some station from the way the refined and polished lady was looking at her in a familiar and intimate manner.

"Ehh . . ." Nora looked at him with a bit of alarm in her eyes, and it occurred to him that he had not even given her his name.

Warrington, presumably, stepped forward to rectify that situation. "I'm Warrington and this is my wife, the Duchess of Warrington." He settled a hand under his wife's elbow. "And you are, sir?"

"Sinclair." He inclined his head. "Constantine Sinclair."

"Oh! Colonel Constantine Sinclair?" The duchess perked up. "How delightful." She looked to Nora. "Are you not delighted, Nora? It's your Colonel Sinclair whom you've been writing to all these years!"

Your Colonel Sinclair.

Nora looked perfectly horrified at her sister's choice of words.

He sank back on his heels and stared hard at the girl who gaped almost comically, her mouth clearly searching for words. Obviously she had no defense.

She had duped him. Mystery solved. Nora had been the one writing to him, pretending to be the late Dr. Langley. He didn't understand why or to what end, but he vowed he would soon have an explanation from her.

"It was you? You've been writing to me?" he demanded, taking a step toward her and then stopping. Angry as he was, he did not wish to appear a charging bull. It was undignified and conduct he did not imagine fitting as Birchwood's heir.

Her cheeks pinked up. "Yes," she admitted.

He shook his head in disgusted awe. "All this time I thought it was Dr. Langley with whom I corresponded. Foolish, I suppose," he said tightly, "to have made that assumption as each letter was signed *from Dr. Langley.*"

She winced at his derisive tone and gave a single resolved nod. "It is true. I signed Papa's name."

"You what?" the duchess exclaimed. "Oh, Nora. You didn't!"

"The colonel wrote asking for some medical advice." She shrugged, and that lighthearted action only inflamed his temper. For her this had been some little thing. An inconsequential game. Only for him, it was no game. For him it was a matter of life and death. Standing here, the hope he had placed in locating Dr. Langley withered a bitter end.

She continued, "Papa had died already, but I knew what to say . . . and how to respond to the colonel's questions, and it was ever so much easier to reply as Papa. I didn't expect a stranger would heed the advice of the late doctor's daughter." Her lips twisted a little as though she had firsthand experience with this.

"Indeed," he muttered, feeling . . . *betrayed*. Perhaps it was not the most fitting descriptor, but it felt accurate nonetheless. For years now, he had penned letters to this female, believing he was communicating with a medical professional, a kind and elderly gentleman concerned with bringing goodness into the world by healing and saving lives. Constantine had been friendly. After a time, he had shared things. Details of himself and his inner thoughts . . . the hardships of living in strange lands, of taking orders without blinking, of leading soldiers into uncertainty, always under the cloud of danger.

None of it embarrassing precisely. He was embarrassed only now. She had made a fool of him. He'd believed he was writing to one person and in fact it had been *her*.

For years he had watched soldiers writing their letters over campfires to their sweethearts, to their families and friends back home. He had never had anyone to write to before. There had never been anyone out there who expected to hear how Constantine Sinclair was managing through life—*if* he was managing at all. Until Langley. And that had turned out to be a lie.

Nora Langley (as he now knew her to be) turned her gaze back on him, and it was full of fiery challenge. "Admit it. What merit would you have given a young girl's words on medical matters?" Was that a sneer in her voice? Directed at him? As though he had done something wrong here.

He stared back at her with her no small amount of incredulity.

Not even an apology for her deceit?

Not the faintest amount of repentance?

She was like no young lady he had ever met . . . certainly not like the gracious and properly circumspect Lady Elise whom he had spent much time with of late. No, Lady Elise was a paragon of virtuous womanhood compared to this.

Nora Langley had all the tenacity of a bulldog. She might be attractive with curves that appealed to many a man, but he could not stomach the sight of her knowing the treachery she had wrought. Presently he would prefer the company of a bulldog rather than face off with this unpleasant female.

"I admit nothing as I have no way of knowing what I would have done." He did his best to get the words out with equanimity, revealing none of his ire. "I was never presented with the truth of the situation, was I?"

"Oh, Colonel." The Duchess of Warrington clasped her hands together before her. "You have our deepest apologies. We so regret any inconvenience this has caused you."

Inconvenience, indeed. He held up his hand. "No need." He'd say anything to escape this drawing room and these people. At any rate, the duchess owed him no apology. The person who owed him an apology had yet to give one. "And I am no longer *Colonel* Sinclair, Your Grace. I've retired my commission and returned home."

"I thought you were in for life? You claimed no interest in leaving the army." Nora Langley looked at him as though he had somehow played a trick on her. Ironic, considering she was the proven liar here. Not him.

"Nora," the duchess chided tightly under her breath. "Don't pester our guest with prying questions." Constantine supposed the tight smile fixed to her face was meant to look natural.

"I've had a change in . . . circumstance. I suddenly find myself heir to my father's cousin. I was called home after the death of his sons."

"Oh, such a tragedy." The duchess sank down on the sofa with a properly contrite expression. "I'm very sorry to hear of your family's loss."

Nora gave a stiff nod of agreement. "Indeed. Very sorry to hear that, Mr. Sinclair."

He acknowledged their words with a nod of his own.

Then the duke was speaking now. "What brings you here now, Mr. Sinclair?" The man was clearly intent on getting to the heart of the matter. "Is there something we might help you with?"

"Well, I've returned to England a few months past to find my cousin's wife suffering from a mysterious ailment. She has seen several doctors, all to no avail."

"Oh, dear." The duchess shook her head. "How dreadful. To lose her sons and then be afflicted so."

"She has had to endure much," he agreed. "I hate to see the duchess in such anguish."

"Duchess?" Warrington queried.

Of course it would come out. It's who he was now. He didn't revel in announcing his new rank, but he supposed it was unavoidable. "My father's cousin is the Duke of Birchwood."

"Oh, my." The Duchess of Warrington's eyes went round. "Then you are . . ."

"The heir to the Duke of Birchwood," Warrington finished.

"Save me from another blasted duke," Nora Langley muttered, almost too quiet for him to hear, but he was standing the closest to her. He heard her perfectly.

"Yes," he allowed. "I am all they have left. And I want to help the duchess. I need to help . . ." He stopped. "I cannot abide to see her suffering. I had thought to fetch Dr. Langley. I can see now I should have sent word first." God knew what kind of reply he would have gotten? The truth? Finally? No. She would have put him off with more lies. "I am sorry to have imposed." He moved toward the door, eager to take his leave. "I won't take up any more of your time." *Or mine.* He turned to go.

"What are her symptoms?" the young Miss Langley asked abruptly.

He stopped and looked back at her. "I beg your pardon?"

"You mentioned this woman is suffering? In what manner?"

He looked from her to the duke and duchess. They did not seem surprised at Miss Langley's question. "I don't want to take up any more of your valuable time . . ." Or further waste his own.

"You came here for help." She looked up at him with wide guileless eyes. "Permit me to help you then."

"Nora is quite the healer, Mr. Sinclair. You've come all this way. You might as well sit with her for a spell before turning around and going home again. There is nothing Nora enjoys more than drowning herself in a mystery diagnosis. She is quite clever." The Duchess of Warrington motioned at Nora with a gentle smile. "Perhaps you two should take a stroll and discuss it."

He did not have time for this. "Oh, I really should get back—"

Warrington strode across the drawing room and opened a door leading out into the gardens. He motioned for Constantine and the young Miss Langley to venture outside.

With a terse nod, he gestured for her to pre-cede him. He'd oblige the duke and duchess and then break away at the first opportunity. All was not forgiven or forgotten and he had no intention of paying heed to anything this charlatan had to say. He'd put all his hopes in coming here . . . and they'd been most miserably dashed.

She swept past him and he followed, closing the doors after them. He didn't glance back at the duke and duchess. He expected it was the last time he would ever see them. Just as this was the last time he would ever see Miss Langley.

He had no room in his life for the likes of her.

Chapter 6

$\mathcal{N}$ora strolled sedately through the gardens with Sinclair beside her, a veritable sycamore tree. She was accustomed to people towering over her. She was the shortest of her three sisters, and there weren't many adults who did not stand above her. It should not have unnerved her that she had to tilt her head back to look up at him, but then everything about this man unsettled her—ever since she had dropped in on him at the pond.

And it turned out he was her Colonel Sinclair.

No. Not *her* colonel. He was not *her* anything. Only her nightmare come to life. She snorted. Indeed, that he was.

She had looked forward to his letters over the years. Above all her other correspondence, there had been something special about his communications. Excitement had thrummed through her when she tore through his envelopes and unfolded the crisp parchment to read his heavy scrawl.

Colonel Sinclair always took the time to share something of himself, where he was, how he and his men were spending their days. He could paint pictures with his words. His description of the rugged mountains of Greece and, more recently, the lush jungles of Bengal Duars, had fed her soul.

Confronted with the reality of him now: young and virile and handsome and heir to a dukedom . . . was jarring. She had thought the personal details, the humor and wit in those letters originated from a crusty old soldier. The mistake was hers. He had never stated his age. She had simply assumed. Incorrectly assumed.

She should never have carried on for so long with him. She had corresponded with others while also pretending to be Papa. It had seemed harmless and become a rather ordinary thing, penning letters and signing his name. An ordinary thing, but something she now keenly regretted.

Sinclair didn't speak. His gaze scanned the gardens as though searching for something . . . an escape perhaps. He had wanted to leave. Her sister and Warrington had put a stop to that, however, and thrust her upon him.

Tension vibrated from him. His anger with her was palpable. She cleared her throat, determined to try and set matters to rights between them. She supposed she owed him an apology. She had not managed that yet. Marian had apologized as though *she* had been the perpetrator and not Nora. That stung a bit.

As the youngest, Nora was accustomed to her sisters speaking for her whether she wished it or not. Of course, she usually did not wish it, but they had been doing that all her life, much to her annoyance. Her pride smarted every time, but there was naught she could do. This instance was no different.

She drew a great breath. Admitting when she was wrong wasn't her strong suit. She knew that weakness of herself, but she would do this.

"I am sorry for my deception. I never imagined I would be confronted—"

"With the evidence of your deceit," he bit back.

Heat flushed through her. "I never imagined my actions would harm anyone."

He said nothing for a long moment and a quick glance revealed the taut lines of his face. Her words had not appeased him. In fact, they might have angered him more if the dull red creeping up the planes of his cheeks was any indication.

She cleared her throat. "I would like to be of

help to you . . . and to your duchess. That is why you came all this way, after all," she reminded him, pausing for a breath and studying him, gauging his reaction. "Of course, nothing quite compares to visiting a patient in person and performing a proper examination, but if you could relay her symptoms to me along with the duration—"

"Forgive me," he cut in, his voice tight with exasperation. "But I find myself with limited trust when it comes to you. I have no intention of discussing the Duchess of Birchwood's private health matters with you. I should like her to live, after all."

"Oh!" *Wretched man!* She stopped and glared at him. "I know what I'm about, sir!"

The look he bestowed on her could turn water to ice. "What right have you to misrepresent yourself?" He sliced a hand through the air. "To lead people astray dispensing medical advice?"

"My advice is not faulty." She resisted stomping her foot in childlike pique.

"No? Who's to say?" He shrugged. "How would I know?"

"I'm not an amateur. You consulted with me for years. Since I—"

"Was a babe in swaddling?" he finished with spiteful flourish.

"Oh!" She gasped at that gibe to her apparent

youth. True, she had been an adolescent when they first began writing to each other, but she was no child. Not then. Not now. She had just turned twenty.

Papa had oft teased that she had *never* been a child, that she had come directly into this world wide-eyed and ready to work alongside him. An old soul, he had called her. "Did you have any issue with anything I imparted to you in my correspondence?"

He pressed his lips together in a mutinous line. "As you well know, most of my inquiries were superficial in nature."

She gawked at him. "Are you that unwilling to give me even the smallest amount of credit?"

"Much of our letters was personal," he flung out, his eyes snapping darkly.

She hesitated, pondering that and realizing it was indeed true. He might have reached out initially with medical questions, but their correspondence had developed into something much more casual and friendly in nature.

She considered him carefully, noting the muscle ticking angrily in his jaw. He was indeed heated over her deception, and she realized it was partly due to this. He felt betrayed.

"Are you a trained physician?" he challenged.

His very question squashed her flash of guilt.

Given that females were not permitted to attend medical schools in Britain, she did not think that to be a fair question. She would have to travel abroad to France or America if she wished to become a physician, and only if she were accepted into a medical college there. She was no stranger to the difficulties such a task presented. Few women, even abroad, were admitted into medical schools.

She pursed her lips before replying, "It's not so easy for my sex. Women are not permitted to be doctors . . . but I trained beside my father for years. I may not be a doctor, but I'm no amateur either. I have skills and—"

"How many?" He nodded once, prompting her to answer.

"How many what?" she asked with a sense of wariness.

"How many others have you written to pretending to be your father? How many others have you duped?"

Oh. She shifted the weight on her feet. "You make it sound criminal."

"I am no legal expert, but I am fairly certain it *is* criminal. At the very least it's immoral."

She lifted her chin in defiance, refusing to let him shame her. It was easy for him to judge. The man was the heir to a dukedom. He could do anything or be anything. He would not know limitations.

If she lived in a different world, if she had been born a man, she would have applied and been admitted to medical school. As a little girl she had once wanted that. She had foolishly thought it was a future she could claim for herself . . . before Papa had explained to her that such things did not happen. He'd told her his own alma mater, Middlesex, would never admit a female. Nor would any of the other medical schools in the kingdom.

"I'm *helping* people. I was helping *you* and everyone else I corresponded with. You took my advice, superficial though it may have been. Do not deny it."

"Fortunately none of your advice has killed anyone . . . that we are aware."

"It has not," she replied in outrage. "I have not killed anyone!"

"How many?" he pressed again, returning to his earlier question. "How many others have you been corresponding with whilst pretending to be your father?"

"Oh." Several moments slid by before she finally, reluctantly, answered. "Three." Then, she grudgingly added, "Maybe ten."

"Ten?" His incredulity succeeded in embarrassing her, despite her personal avowal to not let this man shame her. "This madness must stop, Miss Langley."

She nodded once, petulantly, despising the way he pronounced her name—so very crisply and correctly. As though he were an exasperated schoolmaster or aggrieved governess.

And yet he was correct. She knew that now.

It had to stop. No more corresponding as Papa.

She had never considered that it would come back around to plague her. Perhaps it was short-sighted and foolish, but she had not imagined any adverse consequences to her actions. She saw only that she was able to help people beyond Brambledon. She'd never had that kind of reach before, and it had gone to her head.

She did not want someone else showing up on her doorstep. She would have to content herself with treating the denizens of Brambledon. At least that did not involve duplicity.

He sighed and dragged a hand through his hair. "Do not count on me to keep your deception and trickery a secret."

She canted her head, wariness creeping over her. "What are you saying?"

"I referred you to several of my fellow officers. Durham? He's an army surgeon."

She nodded once, recalling him. "Yes."

"Do you correspond with him?"

"Yes," she admitted, dragging the word out slowly. "We have exchanged a few letters over the years."

"Of course. I am responsible for that. You've made me complicit in your deceit. I must write to all and sundry and inform them that they've been receiving advice from a charlatan."

"No!"

"Yes."

"Why, you—you spiteful—"

"If I am full of spite, Miss Langley," he cut in, his voice sharp as a whip, "it is because I have been duped by a fraud." He stepped close, invading her space with all his crackling anger. "I have wasted precious time to come here and see you when I could have been locating someone who could actually help the Duchess of Birchwood and ease her suffering."

"If you would only tell me what ails her, I could be that someone to help her. Perhaps you could take me to see her and—"

"Are you mad?" He let loose one harsh burst of laughter.

"You know I'm not ignorant when it comes to medical matters. Think back on our letters. Did I never once supply you with useful information?" she challenged.

"Right now I prefer to forget them."

"A woman can know things." She squared her shoulders, hot indignation burning through her, eating at her composure. "We are not merely decorative creatures. We can be more than wives a-and brood mares!"

His dark eyebrows winged high. "I don't doubt the intelligence of women . . . I merely doubt *your* integrity. And as for your knowledge, I do not trust in it."

A hissed breath escaped her.

He continued, "As soon as I reach London, I shall be writing to Durham and all those I once recommended you to so that no one else falls victim to your trickery." He held aloft a finger. "Perhaps I'll even write to your local lord mayor and let him know of the deceiver he has in his community."

"You'll . . . expose me?" She flattened a hand against her chest. She had not thought . . . not imagined . . .

"For the protection of all, yes." He scanned the gardens again, clearly moving on in his mind from thoughts of her. He had no concern at the effect of his words. He would ruin her. He thought her that deserving of that. "Is there a gate where I might exit from the garden?" He only wanted to leave in the speediest way possible.

Her mind whirred, her heart racing. If he destroyed her reputation at Brambledon and no one came to her for her services, then what would she have? What would she do with herself? *What would she be?*

Heavens, the village might have to get an actual doctor to replace her father if they no longer had faith in her.

"Oh, you sanctimonious prig!"

He scanned the garden anew, seemingly indifferent to her accusation as he searched. "Ah. I see a gate. Well then." He looked back at her.

Her reputation as a healer in these parts meant everything to her. She could not lose that. He could not take that from her. She had to find a way to stop him.

He gave a curt wave. "I'm away then."

She glared at him—not that it appeared to affect him. He turned smartly on his heels. She scowled after him, loathing warring with a sharp sense of desperation inside her.

She had to prove to him that she knew what she was about. Then he would forget all about her subterfuge. He would forget and forgive and she could go on as normal with her reputation intact.

Chapter 7

Constantine was intercepted at the front of the grand house. His hopes of slipping away without having to encounter another member of the household were dashed, unfortunately.

"Sinclair," Warrington hailed, stepping in front of him. Clearly the man had been lying in wait, knowing he would depart through the garden.

Constantine peered rather desperately over the man's shoulder in the general direction of the stables, his desired destination. His usual equilibrium fluttered like frayed ribbons in the wind. Coming here had been a mistake. A colossal waste of time. The doctor was dead and he'd been corresponding with a charlatan all this time.

The betrayal cut keenly.

The Duke of Warrington clapped a hand on his shoulder in a gesture that felt somewhat forced. Constantine stared at the hand and then looked back at the man's face.

"You are not leaving so soon, are you?" Warrington inquired.

"That was my intention, yes, Your Grace." There was nothing here for him, after all.

"You must stay the night. Half the day is lost already. Stay and you can leave at first light. It's the sensible plan."

The last thing he wanted was to be stuck beneath the roof with this family. He could ride a few hours and then stay the night at an inn. At least there he would not be forced to talk to anyone and make pleasantries.

"I would not want to impose—"

"Nonsense! No imposition."

Constantine studied the man's face, wondering why it mattered so much to him where he stayed the night. Certainly he did not care.

Warrington's gaze skittered away from him toward the house. Constantine tracked his gaze where it rested on a window. Framed within that window stood the duchess, looking on the sight of them with a hopeful expression.

Of course, the duke's lovely wife had put him

up to this. For whatever reason, she wanted Constantine to stay the night.

"Let us ply you with fine food and a comfortable bed. You'll not find that at any nearby inns. Cook trained in France. It is the least we can offer you after coming all this way to only be met with disappointment."

He was making a strong argument. Constantine enjoyed fine food. Living in a tent and eating food prepared over a campfire had given him an intense appreciation for tasty fare.

Warrington nodded toward the house. "Come now. You can rest in your chamber until dinner. We'll leave you in peace." He pressed a hand to his heart. "You've my vow on that. I'll see to it that no one disturbs you until then."

He looked sharply at the nobleman. Was Constantine so very easy to read then? Did he have a sign looped about his neck declaring himself anxious to be rid of this place and, most notably, Miss Nora Langley?

"Very well. I cannot refuse such a generous offer of hospitality." He would not wish word getting back to Birchwood that he refused the hospitality of a peer. He was trying to prove himself a fitting heir, after all.

"Splendid." The duke motioned him toward the house. "Let's get you settled then."

IF NORA THOUGHT having dinner with Mr. Sinclair might work in her favor, she was mistaken. There was no softening of him toward her. He sat stiff lipped, largely ignoring her as they dined. He spoke to Marian and Nathaniel, but not Nora. Oh, if she asked a direct question of him he would offer a monosyllable response. No more than that. The barest courtesy was only extended to her. Eventually she gave up and finished her meal in silence, attempting to not pout so obviously.

She understood he was displeased with her, but how was she to win him over if he would not speak to her? From the way he avoided even looking at her, she knew he was still angry and as determined as ever to expose her to Durham and the others. He'd said as much and gave no indication that he had changed his mind.

They retired to the drawing room after dinner. Her brother-in-law was not one of those men who abandoned his wife at the first opportunity. Quite the opposite. They spent their evenings together . . . and even much of their days. They sincerely enjoyed each other.

Warrington occupied the sofa beside Marian, smiling at her in his usual besotted fashion as she regaled them with a tale of Mrs. Pratt's pig that once invaded their garden. It was a story that largely featured Nora as she had been the one to straddle the beast and ride it back home to their neighbor.

In fact, most of Marian's stories this evening had revolved around Nora. She frowned. Amusing anecdotes all with Nora at the center.

Marian's laughter eased. "That's our Nora. Intrepid as the day is long."

Sinclair dutifully followed Marian's gaze to Nora. Despite her sister's rousing affirmation, his eyes remained coolly unmoved.

Nora sat ramrod straight on the sofa, trying to appear natural beneath their scrutiny.

Marian reached for her glass, but something happened. She lost her grip. It slipped ever so slightly, spilling her drink down the front of her gown. "Oh, clumsy me!" she exclaimed as her husband quickly claimed a napkin for her.

Warrington helped her to her feet. Ever the gentleman, Mr. Sinclair rose to his feet, too.

"Oh, please, don't get up." Marian waved one hand in reassurance while she settled her other hand on her husband's arm. "Stay. Finish your drink. Nora will keep you company."

Nora stifled a groan. Her sister was the height of obvious. Ever since she had married, ever since Charlotte had married, she had been incorrigible, pelting man after man at Nora. Her matchmaking efforts were unsubtle.

Only Nora could not believe her sister was attempting matchmaking now with Sinclair. The man was scarcely civil to her.

The door thudded shut after them, and it was Nora, Sinclair and the footman in the corner.

Silence fell.

Sinclair looked none too pleased, but that would be no different than how he looked in general . . . at least in their short acquaintance.

She sat in the swelling silence, trying not to let the awkwardness of the moment overtake her. No easy task when her sister and brother-in-law abandoned her to the company of Sinclair in what was an obvious attempt at matchmaking.

She rubbed her sweating palms on her skirts. Sweating palms was a physiological reaction to a stressful situation. Nora supposed this qualified. Sweaty palms. Dilated eyes. Irregular breathing. Nausea even. Yes, yes, yes, yes. At least she wasn't retching at his feet.

She breathed in and out slowly, trying to ease her nerves.

She glanced to the liveried footman. Danny, she believed his name. He stared ahead, not glancing at them, acting as though he was oblivious to their very existence, but, of course, he was not. Of course, he was listening to their every word and would no doubt report it all later below stairs to those who were interested.

Perhaps Marian was not attempting to matchmake. Nora considered this. It was rather extreme, after all, to imagine herself with a duke. Nora would be the first to declare such a thing absurd. Unfortunately, her sister did not recognize that. Apparently she thought a handsome, virile duke was within Nora's reach.

Nora dipped her head to hide her smirk. It would be easier for Nora to rope the moon than snare the heir to a dukedom. Even if she wanted to . . . which she resoundingly did not.

Marian could accomplish such a thing. She *had* accomplished it, after all, because she was Marian. It was within *her* reach—obviously. With her beauty and grace, Marian naturally slid into the role of duchess. She'd actually served as a companion to a duke's daughter for a time before Papa died and she had to return home. Marian knew how that world functioned.

Nora did not know or care to know. She actually chafed against the binds of this life and it wasn't even her life. Not really. This was Marian's life. Nora was merely included in it.

Perhaps Marian was not matchmaking as much

as attempting to soothe over Sinclair's ruffled feathers. *By leaving him alone with me?*

Nora almost giggled at that. She was not known for her charming disposition. It usually did not take a gentleman long to make his excuses and leave her company.

Sinclair had not hidden how very aggrieved he was over her deception. Marian had tried to reassure him, little good it had done. He'd not disguised his contempt of her during their garden stroll.

A glimpse of motion drew her attention back to him as he lifted his glass for a drink. She watched him, the way his throat moved, tendons working in the lamplighst. He drank deeply, as though trying to empty his glass. Of course he was anxious to take his leave.

Why should he be any different from any other gentleman she ever met?

Heavens knew he was eager to make his escape. When he'd left her in the gardens she thought he would be leaving then.

But he'd remained. Now she had a second chance at him. A second chance to change his mind about her before he ruined her reputation and the only patient she would be allowed to treat in Brambledon would be the random chicken.

Charm, however elusive for her, was something she was going to have to implement. She cleared her throat. "What made you decide to stay, Mr. Sinclair?" She fixed a smile to her face.

He stared at her thoughtfully as though debating whether or not he would answer her.

Speak. Please speak. It would only heighten the awkwardness if he chose to ignore her.

At last, his voice filled the air between them. "Your brother-in-law can be very persuasive."

"Nathaniel?" She blinked in some surprise. Nate had gone after him and convinced him to remain? Why had he done that? What had he said? He was not a garrulous sort, and she hardly thought he cared enough about Sinclair to make such an effort to keep him here.

"Yes. Although I believe he was prompted by your sister."

"Ah." That, she could believe. Nathaniel would do just about anything for her. "I think it's more accurate to say my *sister* is persuasive."

"I did spot her through the window looking rather hopeful as he invited me."

"There you have it." She nodded. It was all Marian's doing.

"Well, I don't know how to feel about that."

"What do you mean? Because Warrington was nudged into inviting you for the night?" She shrugged. "Do not most wives control the guest lists?"

"I suppose. I don't have a wife."

"Allow me to enlighten you then. The lady of the house controls all. At least socially."

"If it was important to your sister that I spend the evening here, why has she abandoned me to your tender clutches?"

Obviously Nora couldn't reveal her suspicions—that her sister was playing matchmaker. She shot a furtive look at the silent footman, bothered that he was a silent witness to their conversation.

"Danny?" she inquired.

His gaze snapped to her face. "Miss?"

"Leave us please."

His gaze shifted uncertainly to Sinclair before looking back at her. "Begging your pardon?"

"Please leave us."

"Are you certain—"

"Quite." She nodded, and then watched in silence as he turned and exited the room.

"I don't think that was necessary," Sinclair murmured once they were alone.

"And risk you airing the matter of my . . . charade?"

"Charade?" He released a rough bite of laughter. "That's a delicate phrasing of your dishonesty, but you needn't have worried." He motioned around the fine drawing room. "I am rather new to all of this, but I know to watch what I say in front of the servants. I won't expose your fraud. Yet."

Yet. The word fell heavily on the air, the threat as alarming as ever.

She resisted the urge to defend her actions. She had already attempted that and it had not dissuaded him.

"Ah. Yes." She fixed her smile in place once again. "You find yourself in the enviable position of being heir to a duke."

"I don't know if I would call it enviable. It took the premature deaths of my three cousins for me to become heir."

Had she mentioned she lacked charm? She closed her eyes in a long miserable blink.

"Well, now I feel perfectly wretched."

He grunted in a way that sounded very . . . self-satisfied.

She narrowed her eyes. "But that was your intention, was it not? To keep me in the box where you have allocated me."

"I don't understand your meaning. What box do you speak of?"

"The box where you relegate things you dislike. I am sure I exist in this box for you."

He blinked and shook his head in bewilderment. "I don't . . ."

"Let's see." She angled her head and started counting on her fingers. "My box contains mottled sheep liver. And jellied quail eggs. Warrington's cook has introduced me to both and I wish I had never tasted the like."

He stared at her without expression.

"Do you care for jellied quail eggs?" she asked.

"I can't say I've had the pleasure."

"But you've had the pleasure of me." And he did not like her. Not anymore. Not since realizing she was not her father.

He was staring at her rather oddly now, his dark eyes gleaming. She angled her head, wondering at the sudden intensity of his stare. Then she heard her own words. *You've had the pleasure of me.* They hung in the air between them. Heat crept up her face.

"I have not," he began slowly, "had the pleasure of you."

She nodded briskly, regretting that she had said something that could be interpreted so luridly. She decided not to acknowledge it and changed the subject.

"We've not rubbed on well today." Was it only today that they first came face-to-face? This day felt like it would never end.

He gave a grunt of agreement.

She continued, "You would think we would. We've been corresponding for years."

His reply came quickly. "That wasn't you."

"It was me." She patted her chest. "Those letters were me. They were you and me and we were friends. I might have signed Papa's name, but that is the truth."

He didn't reply. The moments ticked by and his silence was answer enough. He set his glass down with a sharp click. "It grows late."

It was not. Not really. But it was clear he didn't want to be alone with her anymore. She nodded stiffly. "It has been a long day."

"Indeed, it has." He stood and performed a brief bow.

She looked up at him, wondering if she would see him in the morning again, but somehow sensing she would not.

He left her alone in the room.

Danny soon returned and she rose to her feet, knowing he was likely waiting for her to quit the drawing room so that he could make for his bed.

"Good night," she murmured, passing the footman as he moved to kill the lamps.

Bea was waiting for her in her chamber. Nora did not even protest as the maid assisted her in readying for bed. She was too weary to argue the point.

Settled in her comfortable bed, she endured a restless night, plagued by dreams in which she was shunned by the entire village. At one point Nora was walking down the main thoroughfare and several of the villagers were tossing rocks at her. It was a montage of faces. Even Papa was there, frowning in disapproval as he cast stones at her, pelting her in the face and chest. She whimpered, willing him away. Then Sinclair was there, a stone ready to fly in his hand.

She lurched upright in bed in the murky air, gasping, her hand brushing over her face as though she could still feel the sting of sharp rocks.

She swung her legs around and dropped down on the floor, her toes sinking into the plush rug. She sat at the edge of her bed for several moments, breathing heavily, in and out, in and out, before she stood and strode across the chamber to her window. She pushed aside the damask drapes and peered out at the breaking dawn.

There, etched against the softening gray of the impending morning, was a horse and rider, cantering away, leaving Haverston Hall behind.

He'd roused himself and left before the inhabitants of the house were even stirring. It made sense. He'd wanted to leave yesterday. He didn't want to have to see her again.

She watched as he grew smaller and smaller, soon just a speck in the distance, and wondered at the strange tightness in her chest. She let the drapes fall back with a whisper, her hand stroking down the fabric.

Nora would see him again. She vowed it.

Chapter 8

*I*t did not take Nora long to formulate a plan. That was what she did, after all. Her life consisted of plans. She created strategies and carried out experiments to meet hopefully satisfactory end results. That was what she did. Every day.

She intended to propose her plan at dinner that evening to her sister and brother-in-law. She knew that would be the first hurdle—gaining her sister's agreement. Once she had Marian on her side, Warrington would approve. He was besotted with Marian, after all. He'd do anything she asked.

They were on to the second course by the time Nora found her voice. "I've decided to accept Mr. Sinclair's invitation," she proclaimed as she reached for her glass of claret and took a fortifying sip.

The clatter of cutlery around the table stopped abruptly.

Marian and Nathaniel exchanged a long look. They did that often. Nora supposed married couples did that sort of thing. She could not recall if her parents ever did. She held so few memories of her mother, unfortunately. She'd died when Nora was young. She always envied that Marian and Charlotte had had more time with her, more memories to reflect upon.

And now Marian had Nathaniel. And Charlotte had Kingston.

They were forming their own families, building their own lives without her. She tried not to feel jealous, and she truly wasn't. Not precisely. She simply felt left behind. They'd moved on with the next stage of their lives and left her behind. Not forgotten. Some days she felt that it would be easier if they did forget her. Then they would not attempt all their subtle and not-so-subtle efforts to see her married off to whatever gentleman of the hour struck them as eligible. Really. It was like they didn't know her at all if they thought she could be tempted by the banality of domesticity.

"What invitation?" Marian inquired after some

moments, lowering her forkful of buttered parsnips back down to her plate. "I don't recall that he invited you anywhere."

"Indeed," Warrington seconded, looking equally bewildered. "I don't recall an invitation being extended either." Naturally, he would support his wife.

"Oh, he did during our walk through the gardens." She fluttered a hand vaguely, hoping she did not appear dishonest—even if she was. *Especially* because she was. "He came here for my help, after all—"

"*Your* help?" Warrington looked at her dubiously.

"He did not come here for you. He came here for help from *Papa*," Marian reminded pointedly, waving her fork in a small circle. "He did *not* extend that invitation to you, Nora. He did not even leave without saying farewell. Merely spoke to Mrs. Conally and asked her to pass along his compliments and appreciation to us." She made a face, pursing her lips as though she had bitten into something particularly sour. "I had hoped when I left you with him you might have softened him."

"Yes, that did not work."

Marian sighed with a rueful shake of her head, her hand lowering to rub her generous belly. "I suppose I should have known better. You're not known for your charm."

That bit of truth stung. For once she wished she had Marian's gifts so she could have enchanted Sinclair to the point that he forgot his displeasure with her. She frowned at the wishful thought. It felt a betrayal to herself. She was not like Marian and Charlotte and she had never longed to be.

With indignation stewing inside her, she grumbled, "I would have softened him if he only believed me when I told him that I learned all my skills from Papa and I am perfectly capable of helping him."

"Well, I think we can put that hope aside. According to Mrs. Conally he seemed quite cross and eager to depart." Marian calmly returned her attention to her food.

"I think the most important thing to remember here," Nora said with heavy emphasis as she moved her fork aimlessly in her buttered parsnips, "is that the Duchess of Birchwood needs help and I am equipped to give her that assistance."

"You know nothing of this woman's condition so you cannot know if you can help her or not," Marian pointed out very reasonably. Always so very reasonable. That was frustrating. Even now that they were older, Marian still treated Nora as though she were frozen in childhood. Her sisters had grown into women who married and entered motherhood, but Nora was stuck as a child.

"Certainly the duchess has the finest physicians in London at her disposal," Warrington added unhelpfully. There was also a roundabout insult buried in there. Of course if the duchess had the best doctors available to her, there was nothing that Nora could offer her.

"And yet he came here looking for *me*," Nora stated.

"For Papa," Marian inserted. "He does not need or want you."

Nora's temper sparked. She would always be that bothersome little sister in Marian's eyes. Emphasis on the world *little*. "But should I not see her and make that assessment for myself? You know I am good at what I do. I'm not making that up," she challenged.

Marian nodded grudgingly. "Indeed, you are."

"I owe Sinclair that after our many years of correspondence. We were friends of a sort—"

"You mean Colonel Sinclair believed himself to be friends with your father," Warrington pointed out as he cut into his pheasant. "Not you."

"London is not a mere rock's skip from here," Marian reminded before Nora had a chance to respond to her exasperating brother-in-law. "The duchess is not a short walk across the shire as with your usual patients."

"I am aware of that."

"Good then. Because obviously I cannot travel in my condition." Shaking her head, she resumed eating as though the matter were closed. "It's much too close to my time." She added a bit of the fig compote to her pheasant-laden fork. "Mmm. Is that cherries with the figs? Delicious."

Warrington nodded. "I was just about to remark the same."

Marian smiled besottedly at her husband.

Nora struggled not to retch.

"It was not my meaning to suggest you have to accompany me," Nora defended. It was actually the last thing she wanted. She could do with some time away from Marian . . . from her entire family for that matter. Considering she had never had a respite from her family *ever*, it was long overdue.

Marian looked up, blinking innocuously. "Then who did you mean to accompany you? Charlotte has her hands much too full with Cordelia."

"I uh . . . I can bring Bea. She should be glad to be of use. She is oft complaining that I don't utilize her nearly enough."

"It does vex her that you forgo her services." Marian shook her head ruefully. "Poor lass."

"Then she should be most glad to accompany me to London and be of use." Nora reached for her glass and drank deeply, counting herself the winner of this skirmish.

Until her sister spoke.

"I'm sorry, Nora. I cannot approve. You've never been to London, and we cannot send you there without one of us to escort you . . . especially to call on a gentleman I am convinced never wants to see you again. He parted here quite ill-tempered. I can hardly release you to his clutches."

"Clutches?" She snorted. "He's not a great clawed harpy, Marian."

"Your sister is quite correct," Warrington agreed, his deep voice carrying across the table. Of course he agreed. "You cannot go down on your own. Even with Bea as a companion, it's not advisable."

Her brother-in-law doted on her sister. He would not naysay Marian on a matter such as this. Doubtlessly, he thought Nora's wishes to go down to London were trivial and therefore easy to dismiss. He couldn't know, couldn't understand, what it meant to her.

Her fingers tightened around her cutlery until her knuckles went white. Their denial felt like a slap—a reminder that she would never be an autonomous person to them . . . to anyone. To the world she was merely Nora Langley, kinswoman to people who mattered but not a person who mattered in her own right.

She might operate under the illusion of independence, but it was just that. An illusion. In moments like this, when reality slapped her in the face, she felt as powerless as a newborn babe.

"Is it merely a trip to London you crave?" Marian asked as she served herself from the platter the footman proffered. "Perhaps we can all go? In a half year?"

We can all go. In a half year.

Again, as though she were a little girl being placated with the promise of a sweet treat. The words only added to her bad temper. *In a half year.* Those words felt as heavy and burdensome as a yoke about her neck. It would be too late by then. Sinclair would have written to Durham and the others. Her good name could very well be ruined even as far as their small shire.

Marian smiled at her in a cajoling manner, perfectly oblivious to Nora's churning emotions.

The footman arrived at Nora's side and she distractedly lifted the serving spoons to serve herself.

Her sister thought her offer perfectly generous. She had no notion of Sinclair's threat to expose Nora's machinations to the world. For some reason Nora did not want to reveal that piece of information, however much it guided her impulse to go after Sinclair. She was certain Marian would be appalled and Warrington would feel compelled to act on her behalf. He would likely leave Marian in her delicate condition and hie off after Sinclair. He'd think it was his duty as her eldest male relation. Her brother was still a lad in school, after all. The last time he'd visited during holiday his voice still cracked when he talked.

It was rather nice, she supposed, to have an older brother to care for her and look after her. She couldn't drag him into her mess.

No, Nora could not have that. It would be just her luck that Marian would give birth whilst Warrington was gone. That was unacceptable. She could not risk that happening. She could not reveal Sinclair's threat and potentially be the reason he missed the birth of his first child.

Her sister was perfectly kind and she had done so much for Nora, for all of them. She had made so very many sacrifices upon Papa's death. Nora would handle this situation herself.

Nora forced a smile. "Perhaps to mark the New Year?" she suggested. "We can all go to Town."

"Splendid," Marian exclaimed. "Charlotte, Kingston and both babies can join us. We shall make an occasion of it. It will be a wonderful family affair. We shall shop and visit the museums and the theaters. You can meet this Duchess of Birchwood and assure yourself of her well-being."

Nora nodded in seeming agreement.

The matter was settled then. At least in Marian's mind it was.

They would travel to London in a half year and Nora would be a good and proper girl in the meantime, sitting on her backside, waiting for the moment her family snapped their fingers and allowed her out into the world.

The matter was settled for Nora, too.

She would be going to London on the first train out tomorrow.

Chapter 9

$\mathcal{N}$ora debated long and hard whether to bring Bea with her despite what she had told Marian and Warrington when she first announced her intention to travel to London. There were advantages and disadvantages to doing such a thing.

Of course, it was advisable to bring a companion with her on the journey. More than advisable. It was propriety and customary at that. Even she, who gave so little regard to what was customary or proper, recognized that.

Nora was not a seasoned traveler either. She had never left the shadow of Brambledon. Naturally she should have a companion with her, but there was still the very real matter of whether or not she could trust Bea.

She was asking a great deal of the maid. Not only to accompany Nora to London . . . but to *not* alert anyone in the house that they were leaving. It was not a small thing to ask—especially considering Warrington was her employer, and Bea was not of a reticent nature. It seemed much too likely the maid would reveal her plan to Marian.

Then Nora's journey would be over before it had ever even started.

Even if Bea agreed, Marian would discover her absence—their absences—and soon. If Nora went alone, Warrington would be after her like an outraged papa.

Nora might have half a day head start at the most before the alert went up that she was gone. And yet Marian would worry less if she knew Bea was with her. There was that.

Taking Bea was her only hope. Plain and simple.

A nicely worded letter pleading her cause and Bea as a proper companion might save her. Marian might not send Warrington after her.

Ultimately, it was this that had her confiding her plans to Bea.

"London?" Bea nodded jerkily as Nora laid forth the details. "Truly? Yes, yes. yes. I will happily accompany you."

Apparently she did not require much convincing.

The maid was so enthused at the prospect of a trip to London and having something to do with her time (finally) that she heartily agreed— with the promise that Nora would prevent her from getting sacked when their adventure was discovered.

"You won't be sacked." Nora hoped she was not mistaken in issuing forth such a promise and it was one she could honor. Certainly Warrington wouldn't punish Bea for traveling with Nora. "Once we reach London, I'll send them a letter and let them know I'm the guest of the Duke and Duchess of Birchwood. They'll be mollified and will dare not come for fear of creating a stir. It's only a scandal if they behave as though I stole away in the night without their permission . . . and reveal that to all and sundry."

At least she hoped so. On all counts. She hoped Sinclair would not toss her out on her ear. She hoped she would be welcomed as a guest of the Duke and Duchess of Birchwood. She hoped her family would not come in hot pursuit of her.

So much of this depended on Sinclair and how he reacted to her arrival.

Bea made quick work of packing Nora's luggage and then disappearing to pack her own things.

They left before dawn, creeping out of the

house like thieves in the dark in time to catch the morning train. Bea arranged for her cousin, Bobby, one of the stable lads, to take them to the station, and that was some comfort to Nora. Who was more trustworthy than family?

Nora tried to contain her excitement as they settled into their seats. She stared out the window up until the very last moment, as though expecting to see a member of her family charging after them on the platform. No one came.

Then they were on their way.

Colonel Sinclair—no, *Mr.* Sinclair—would soon see that whilst she was not Dr. Langley, she was very much his daughter in every sense and a fine and capable healer.

She'd see the duchess through whatever ailed her and he could choke on all his doubts about her.

She stared out the window at the passing countryside, anticipation zipping through her. In a few hours, she would be in London.

IT TURNED OUT locating the residence of the Duke and Duchess of Birchwood was not such a difficult task. Birchwood was not your average duke, it seemed—if dukes could be called average. Nora supposed her sister marrying a duke had somewhat normalized them in her mind.

After lengthy exposure to Warrington, she had removed dukes from their category of mythical figures where she had always allocated them.

It was becoming apparent, however, as she sat on the edge of a brocade settee in the grand Birchwood drawing room under the watchful eye of stone-faced footmen, that the Duke of Birchwood was cut from a different cloth. She'd always thought her brother-in-law maintained a preposterous number of servants, but now, after seeing the amount of staff Birchwood kept on hand, she changed her mind.

As she waited, the moments ticking by, she was reminded that the Duke of Birchwood was not Warrington and she placed dukes back in their previous category alongside mythical figures.

She eyed the elegantly appointed room.

It was not that Haverston Hall was *not* an impressive residence, only that this place, this place where Sinclair lived and would one day be master, seemed much more palatial.

A great many cherubs stared at her from the elaborate gilt molding. And not only there. They were in the many paintings and the vases and the bric-a-bracs sitting on every surface. They were an army and she was surrounded. She could not recall a single cherub at Haverston Hall. Indeed, that place had been austere upon their arrival, virtually devoid of everything except basic furnishings. Marian had been gradually filling the place, making it more of a home . . . but not one with ornate cherubs.

Something existed in the air of Birchwood House. An elusive quality that she felt in the very atmosphere and it had naught to do with the garish cherubs. She attributed the distinction to Warrington, or rather Birchwood.

Whereas Birchwood was an esteemed member of the House, prominent among his peers—her brother-in-law preferred country life and scarcely ever stepped foot in Town.

She smoothed a hand over her skirts, aware of the eyes of the stoic footmen on her. Haverston Hall had its footmen, but she did not recall them standing about like statues, staring straight ahead with eerie intensity.

She cleared her throat. Her dress was a little wrinkled from the long train ride, and she felt unnaturally self-conscious. She wished she'd been able to change her garments and freshen up. She resisted the impulse to touch her hair. She willed herself to at least project an air of confidence.

She was not alone in the room. However much the footmen were trained to appear oblivious to her, she was not oblivious to them.

Nora forced her hands to stillness so she did not appear fidgety and nervous—even if she happened to be. She usually gave very little thought to her appearance, but being in this room made her feel a little out of sorts.

Bea had been escorted somewhere else in the house whilst Nora had been escorted to the drawing room to wait for the arrival of Sinclair. She did not think she would miss the chatter of her maid—it had filled her ears on the long train ride—but she did.

Suddenly Sinclair was there, filling the threshold, larger than even memory served.

His chest lifted on a great inhalation at the sight of her.

She straightened, angling herself to face him better and pasting on a smile. She was determined to begin this exchange on a cheerful note—better than the way they had ended things in Brambledon.

It was not long ago, days only, that they had stood face-to-face, but he seemed *more* than she remembered and she had made quite a thorough study of him at the pond. He'd given her so much to observe, after all. The long line of him. The broad shoulders. That taut, mesmerizing backside.

Today though, standing here in his domain,

he was more mature, more imposing. His unsmiling face sterner.

His dark-eyed scrutiny made her fingers clench around her thighs as though she suddenly needed to hold on to something. She had never found herself the subject of such intense examination.

"Malone? Jones?" His eyes remained fixed on her as he spoke to the footmen. "Could you leave us, please?"

The two footmen left without a word, nodding deferentially to Sinclair as they passed—the man who would one day be master of this place and all within it.

Sinclair closed the drawing room doors after them and advanced into the room. "What are you doing here, Miss Langley?"

She rose from the settee, not appreciating the disadvantage of sitting whilst he stood. She'd get a crick in her neck looking up at him. Circling the settee, she smoothed her hands along the back. "You came to me for help, so I am here to help."

"I left you in Brambledon," he corrected and from his hard tone it was clear that he had expected her to stay there. The man had much to learn about her if he thought her that easy to chase away.

"Well," she said, fighting to keep her tone friendly. "I am not in Brambledon."

"I see that. You followed me."

She inclined her head. "Not immediately, but yes. I followed you here. As I said . . . to help."

"And as I said before, I have little faith that you can help—"

"But you do have a *little* faith," she pointed out playfully.

He scowled.

She took advantage of the pause and continued, "Is the duchess still ill?"

He crossed his arms. "She has her . . . spells. They come and go."

"So I'm to assume she *is* still ill then." His frown was answer enough. "It would be remiss of you *not* to explore every option for her."

"And I'm to assume you consider yourself just such an option?"

"Actually I consider myself your solution, but you should at the very least consider me an option. Or perhaps your devotion to the duchess doesn't run as deeply as you claim." She arched an eyebrow.

He did not care for that suggestion. "You go too far—"

"You vowed to find the duchess some relief from her condition. That being the case, you should not cast out someone capable and willing to help. That seems shortsighted, does it not?"

"Are you capable, Miss Langley?" He angled his head. "Truly? The only thing I have to recommend you is your history of deceit."

Ugh. He was going to hold that over her head forever. "If you had done research you would know of my capabilities, sir. Ask anyone in Brambledon."

"I'm not presently in Brambledon, am I?"

"You were there. You didn't even inquire about my credentials when you were there. I can offer you countless testimonials."

"Admittedly, after discovering I had been duped for years, I was in no mood—"

"So this is about your injured pride then? I thought you were concerned with the well-being of the Duchess of Birchwood. I did not realize this was about you."

He angled his head sharply, his eyes narrowing on her. "Do you think insulting me a way to endear you to me?"

She shrugged. "Again, this is not about me or you . . . or how *you* feel about *me*. It's about a very ill woman."

His lips compressed and she knew she had either made her point—or just gotten herself tossed out of there.

She decided to take a page from her sisters and adopt a conciliatory manner in case she had pushed him too far. "Please, Mr. Sinclair. Let me try. What do you have to lose?"

He stared at her a long time with those deep eyes of his, so dark, so impenetrable. "What do you want out of this?"

She straightened her spine. "What makes you think I want anything?"

"What. Do. You. Want?"

Your respect. She wanted him to look at her and admit he was wrong, that she was as capable as any doctor. Oh, and she wanted to know her reputation as a healer was safe. Healing the duchess was also another factor. Marian was right. She loved nothing more than solving a mystery diagnosis.

"I'd like you to promise not to expose me . . . Don't write to Durham and any of the others."

"Am I to let you continue your lying then?"

"No. I'll write of my father's passing and cease giving out advice in his name." She stared at him hopefully.

He was silent for a moment, considering her with narrowed eyes.

She continued, "Once you see that I can help her, you will realize I know what I'm about. Allow me to treat her." She nodded encouragingly. It was perfectly reasonable. "And I should stay here, of course, as yours and the Birchwoods' guest."

He sputtered. "Have you here? Under this roof?"

"Where else shall I stay in London? I don't know anyone."

"Do you commonly invite yourself to people's homes?"

She frowned. "The only way my sister and Warrington will tolerate me staying in London is to stay here . . . as a guest of the Birchwoods. Anything else would be unseemly."

"Tolerate? Did they not give you leave to venture here?"

Some of her poise evaporated at the question. "Er, no. I slipped away with my maid before they woke."

"Without their permission?"

His question fired her indignation anew. "I'm an adult. I don't require permission."

"And yet you're concerned at what they may or may not *tolerate*."

She glared at him, not liking her own words tossed back at her. "I said I can help her, and so I can." She propped a hand on her hip. "Will you at least show me to her?"

"I . . . ah. I do not know. Her husband is very protective. I do not think he will allow you near her. She's under the care of a most prominent and capable physician. I believe he and the duke attended Eton together."

"Has she improved yet under this most prominent and capable physician?"

"As I said. She has spells."

"So not yet then. It seems to me her physician must not be so very capable if she is still ill."

"You are full of self-confidence, aren't you?"

She shrugged. "Competence begets confidence. Now. Can you be more specific? What are these spells like?"

He looked at her long and hard and for a moment she thought his resolve was cracking and he was truly considering her offer. Then, he shook his head. "I'm sorry. You've come all this way for naught. The duke will not allow you to see his—"

"Sinclair? Is that you in there? It's my understanding that we have a guest." An older gentleman entered the room. He was past middling age but in possession of a full head of glorious white hair. His gaze landed on her. "Ah, you must be the visitor mentioned. Sinclair? Aren't you going to introduce me to the young lady?"

Sinclair looked pained. "Indeed, Your Grace. Allow me to introduce you to Miss Nora Langley. Miss Langley, may I present the Duke of Birchwood."

She executed a curtsey. She'd had some practice since becoming Warrington's sister-in-law. She had seen the courtesy performed countless times.

"A pleasure, Miss Langley. Will you be staying for luncheon? We are to sit down to eat soon. The duchess is having one of her better days. She has roused from her nap and will soon join us."

"That won't be necessary. Miss Langley was just—"

"I should enjoy that. Thank you, Your Grace. I am quite famished from my journey here."

"Journey? And where have you come from, Miss Langley?"

"Brambledon, Your Grace."

"And do you reside there with your . . . family, Miss Langley?" He looked rather pointedly between Sinclair and Nora, and she realized he was inviting an explanation to be given for her appearance in his drawing room and, more specifically, her connection to Sinclair. He wanted her credentials, in short, and to know if her pedigree warranted her a place in his drawing room.

"Yes." She might as well give him what he was seeking, and hoped it achieved the desired result, which was to secure an invitation to stay. "I live in Brambledon with my sister and her husband . . . the Duke of Warrington, Your Grace."

His eyes lit up. "Ah. Warrington? I've heard of the man, I believe." He nodded slowly. "Never met him though. Bit of a recluse, is he not?"

"Yes. Warrington does prefer country living," she allowed.

"Never been much our custom. The duchess has always enjoyed Town." He chortled. "Too many bees in the country, she always says." His smile slipped. He frowned then, presumably at the mention of his wife, as though the reminder of her troubled him greatly. Her mystery illness, no doubt.

The reason she was here. To prove herself.

The duke blinked and his somber mask slipped away. "Well, you must come dine with us and tell me all about yourself and what brings you to Town and how it is this village of Brambledon has so enamored Warrington that he eschews all of Society."

"I believe my sister is the reason behind that. Warrington is quite enamored of *her*. They're awaiting the arrival of their first child and quite content to stay where they are."

"Ah. As should be the case." He released a heavy breath. "A child . . . such a blessing. Such a gift." The somber look returned to his face and Nora was reminded that he had lost his sons, thus making Sinclair his heir and bringing him home.

Home to her.

No, not *to* her. Simply . . . home. Yes, he ended up on her doorstep as a result of returning home, but he had not come home *for* her or *because* of her. She was an incidental.

The duke cleared his throat as though a lump was stuck there.

Sinclair gave her a look of rebuke. An awkward silence swelled among them.

She returned Sinclair's look with a helpless one of her own. It had not been her intention to bring forth painful memories. She had mentioned the arrival of her sister's and Warrington's child only as a topic of conversation.

She opened and closed her mouth several times, searching for something to say to alleviate the sudden somber mood.

"Yes, well, *I* am what brought Miss Langley to London."

The duke's bowed head snapped up, his eyes bright beneath his stark white eyebrows. "What's that?"

She gazed at Sinclair, equally at a loss. "Yes . . . what . . ."

Her words went unheard, or at least unac-
knowledged. Sinclair continued, "I've sent for
Miss Langley and invited her to stay with us.
She's the daughter of the late Dr. Langley, who
was a very talented physician. She trained at his
feet and is an excellent healer in her own right
with a particular forte for pain mitigation."

"Oh." The duke turned back to look at her, assessing her anew.

She valiantly tried to show no reaction to the
praise . . . to not flinch or swallow or blink like
an owl in astonishment that he should laud her
in such a way.

"Well, that is . . . something." The duke nodded slowly, uncertainly, clearly absorbing that
she, a woman, no doubt a *girl* in his estimation,
should possess any medical skill at all. She was
well versed in such disbelief, even though the
residents of Brambledon were largely accepting.
There were always those few. A man of the house
too resistant and guarded to allow her to treat
his womenfolk.

Birchwood dragged a wizened hand through
his lush pelt of white hair.

"It could not hurt to have her here," Sinclair
pressed, gesturing to Nora. "She can assist with
the duchess and see what, if any, relief she might
offer. At the very least the duchess would enjoy

having another lovely reading voice on hand. Her eyes aren't what they used to be and she's quite fond of her books."

She tried not to flinch at that. She was not here to read books out loud.

The duke nodded slowly. "I suppose it could do no harm to have a gentlewoman with her particular skill in . . . what did you call it? Pain . . ."

"Mitigation," Nora supplied.

"Yes. Very good." The duke nodded once and moved in, offering his arm to Nora. "Shall we take a stroll in the garden before luncheon? It shall prepare our constitution. Cook enjoys his rich sauces. Trained in France under the best. He does make a marvelous meringue. We shall have him prepare one while you are here."

She released a breath and accepted his arm, sliding an uncertain glance to Sinclair. She was not sure what to make of him. The last thing she had expected was for him to vouch for her.

Thanks to him she would be staying here.

As she departed the drawing room on the duke's arm, she could not resist looking over her shoulder for a glimpse of him.

He followed at a sedate pace, his dark eyes trained on her face as though he knew she would look back at him again.

He knew she would and he was ready with a look of his own.

He arched an eyebrow over his dark eyes and conveyed an expression full of warning that said: *You've got your chance. Now prove yourself.*

Chapter 10

I think you should wear the peach silk this evening," Bea pronounced. "You were caught unprepared at luncheon yesterday with your dusty travel clothes, but we shall not repeat that faux pas." She tsked and shook her head as though greatly regretting said faux pas. "Not on my watch. This evening you shall look every inch the lady, and an enticing one at that." The maid hung the peach gown on the outside of the wardrobe, smoothing a hand over the skirts that she had already so valiantly worked free of wrinkles.

"I don't think anyone minded," Nora reassured her.

"Oh, it was noted. Trust me. I've spent enough time in the last day downstairs with the rest of the staff, and I can assure you that your state of dress was a point of discussion among those vultures."

Nora fought back a flinch. She did not care what strangers thought of her. If the opinions of strangers mattered to her, she would have fallen in line like a proper soldier and already married. Heavens, she'd likely have a child or two clinging to her skirts.

Bea continued, "Never have I met such a group of hoity-toity servants." She started digging around through the wardrobe, muttering to herself as she examined the slippers she had packed with a frown. "I should have packed more choices. If I had known we were coming to a place like this . . ." Her mutter faded away and she swept her gaze around the bedchamber with an air of accusation.

This chamber had no cherubs, but there were peacocks everywhere. On the vases and paintings. Even the brass table lamps: peacocks, peacocks, peacocks.

"My apologies," Nora said, although she was not certain what she was apologizing for. She could not have known the Duke of Birchwood would live quite so differently from the Duke of Warrington.

Sinclair appeared in her mind. This was all his. This place. This life. For however mismatched

Sinclair and this world seemed in her mind, they went together.

She had never seen Sinclair in uniform, but she better imagined him mud splattered in his colors, striding rigidly across an army field. That seemed more fitting an occupation for him than *dukeing* it about London.

Bea gave a small grunt and lifted a pair of slippers out from the floor of the armoire, attempting to straighten the tiny bows secured at each of the toes. "This will have to do. Don't know what the staff has to be so priggish about. Told them I came from a duke's household, too. Apparently Warrington is not as grand and venerable as Birchwood." She gestured widely around them with an exaggerated air of disgust. "Apparently there is an order even among dukes and our duke is at the bottom of the stack."

That was quite possibly true, but she did not think Warrington cared. In fact, she was certain that he preferred it that way.

"I don't think the Duke or Duchess of Birchwood minded my wardrobe," Nora offered.

The Duchess of Birchwood had joined them at luncheon yesterday, refreshed from her nap. She was perfectly pleasant and delighted that Nora would be staying with them. She had not blinked an eye over Nora's vocation. She even seemed quite eager to try a few of Nora's remedies. Women were always more accepting and open-minded of Nora's efforts.

She had beamed at Nora as she said, "I'm feeling quite improved today, but a week rarely passes without one of my spells. Unfortunately, it won't be long until I take another turn." Her smile diminished a bit at that. "Then we will see what happens and you shall have your hands full with me."

"I am at your disposal," Nora pledged.

"I'm almost looking forward to that." The duchess turned her attention to Sinclair to praise him. "So good of you to send for her, Constantine. At the very least she will be a pleasant diversion."

Nora did not know how she felt about being described as a diversion. It conjured an image of herself sitting in a chair reading beside the ailing lady as she reclined in bed. It felt somehow minimizing. Nora was more than that. She was a healer.

"I only seek your comfort, Your Grace," Sinclair had replied in that subdued manner of his that somehow grated upon Nora's nerves. Could he not display a little emotion? It was . . . unnatural. And did he want to be that? A purveyor of diversions?

He was more than this, too.

At his response, the duchess lowered her spoon back into her bowl with a dissatisfied clink. "Now, now, Constantine. What have I said? We are beyond such formality. You are the Birchwood heir." She said the words with a smile, but there was something in her voice, a certain quaver, a drop in the tone of her voice that betrayed her, that revealed she was not completely unaffected at the significance of Sinclair being the Birchwood heir. The significance being that her offspring were all gone—dead, wiped from the earth by the cruel vagaries of life. "You must call me Maude."

He nodded once, as stiff and austere as ever (he already had this duke thing down), but he did not respond with the vocalization of her Christian name, and Nora somehow doubted he ever would. She rather thought he was incapable of doing that. Such familiarity was beyond the man.

"And what of Mr. Sinclair?" Bea asked, pulling Nora from her reverie.

Nora blinked. "I beg your pardon?"

"Mr. Sinclair?" she prompted, as though she knew of Nora's preoccupation with the man. "The heir? Is he not the reason we came here?"

"No!" she cried in outrage. "Why would you say such a thing?"

"We hared half across the country. I assumed

it was for a man. And as far as men go, he is a fine specimen. What other reason could there be?"

Nora sniffed. "My actions are not motivated by the male species—*fine specimen*, or no."

Bea stared at her with a decidedly unimpressed expression. "It's my experience that all actions of people are motivated by desire."

"That's a little rudimentary. You make us all sound like we live in caves and only care about procreating and our next meal."

Bea arched an eyebrow and lifted a single shoulder in a shrug. "A bit primitive. We're not cavemen precisely, but that's about the right of it. Simple biology, yes? Isn't this your area of expertise?"

Nora shook her head, disliking the notion that they all operated on the same level as instinct-driven cavemen. "We are civilized. With brains in our heads."

"It's not far from the truth. It's fairly simple."

"I agree that it is simple. We're here to help the duchess. *I* am here to help her. This has nothing to do with Mr. Sinclair."

Bea shrugged and then went back to correcting the bows on Nora's slippers. "If you say so."

"I do," she snapped.

Bea gave an apologetic shrug. "A natural misunderstanding on my part. He is young—"

"Is he?" She wrinkled his nose. "He must be at least a decade older than me."

"Still young," she insisted. "I would say about thirty. If you think him old, then that makes you . . . a child. A *woman* would think him quite young and virile. He is most certainly up to the task."

Nora stiffened in affront. She had a fairly good notion to what task Bea referred.

Bea smirked and continued, "As I said, young. And handsome and eminently eligible. He's set to inherit a dukedom. He should very much be the reason you take pains to look your best this evening and every evening you are here. He might be courting this Lady Elise but there have been no official announcements yet. As far as I'm concerned that means he's fair—"

"What did you say?"

"He's fair game as far as—"

"No, before that."

"Oh. He's courting a Lady Elise, who happens to be the daughter of the late Earl of Drafford. She was the earl's only child and is a great heiress. Lovely, too, from all accounts. Accomplished. Kind in temperament from all reports and she was betrothed to the Duke of Birchwood's eldest son. It seems she is determined to be the next Duchess of Birchwood, for she has been quite amenable to Sinclair's suit since he returned to England."

Nora shook her head in wonder. "How do you know all of this? We have been here one day only."

"I said the servants were hoity-toity. I did not say they didn't gossip. They've loose tongues aplenty. They are more than willing to share all the tittle-tattle and a day was plenty of time to do that."

"Evidently."

"Now. Let's ready you for dinner."

"It's over an hour from now."

"We need every moment if I'm to do what I have in mind with your hair."

Nora released a much-beleaguered sigh and allowed herself to be guided to the dressing table.

She'd already enjoyed a bath and was wrapped cozily in a dressing gown. She'd spent most of the day in the company of the duchess. They'd had breakfast and luncheon together, just the two of them. They'd played cards and strolled the gardens. Fortunately for the duchess she was pain-free and quite looking forward to the small dinner party she was hosting that evening.

Nora could do without dinner parties. She would rather get to the matter of healing the duchess, but as the lady exhibited no outward symptoms, she could do nothing more than wait for the next spell.

She had not seen the duke or Sinclair since yesterday. She had resisted prying into the whereabouts of either gentleman when she was with the duchess—a definite test of her will as she was one to usually speak whatever came to her mind. She definitely had to channel her sisters' calm temperaments to hold her tongue. She had no idea what kept the gentlemen away. Doubtlessly, the duke had much to teach Sinclair about his legacy.

Most heirs spent a lifetime training for the role. With three sons, clearly no one had expected Sinclair to inherit. Who had ever been afflicted with such a run of bad luck?

He had been living his own life as a colonel a world away from England. Now he was here, thrust into this new position. She wondered what his feelings were on the matter. He hardly appeared gleeful over his new fate. She suspected he was not enamored with the change of his circumstance, however, he was not one to reveal his emotions.

She sank down on the bench before the dressing table and allowed Bea to work on her hair, telling herself she did not care one way or another with the end result. She was not here to win people over with her appearance, and she was certainly not here to charm Mr. Sinclair. This paragon Lady Elise was welcome to him. He could court and marry whomever he chose. It had naught to do with Nora.

THE DAY HAD been interminable.

Constantine had spent most of it with Birchwood and his man of affairs, Somerton, poring over ledgers and listening to the two older gentlemen reminisce about the days of their youth when both their lives had been bright and shiny, full of possibility. Days when all three of the duke's sons had been alive, spirited boys frolicking through the halls, cheeks flushed and full of life. The specter of death had been nowhere in sight.

Constantine tried not to reveal how awkward he felt in those moments, knowing his very presence was a reminder to the Birchwoods of all they had lost. He would forever represent that to them—loss.

Constantine was a symbol of their grief. It was a heavy burden to bear, and yet he would bear it. He would do his best to honor his lost cousins and the duke and duchess. It was the least he owed to them.

Birchwood glanced at the clock ticking the

seconds above the mantel. "Ah! How time has flown. We'd best adjourn for the day. My dear Maude will not be happy if we are not dressed and ready for dinner on time, Constantine."

He nodded. "Of course, Your Grace."

Birchwood's man of affairs gathered up his books and ledgers and took his leave then with a crisp bow to each of them. Before Constantine could follow him from the room, Birchwood stalled him with a hand on his arm. "A word, please."

Constantine nodded, waiting for the door to click shut behind Somerton. He looked expectantly to the duke.

The man's hand on Con's arm gave an encouraging squeeze. "Lady Elise, as you know, will be in attendance this evening."

"Yes." He nodded, wariness instantly creeping over him. "I'm aware." The duke's gaze grew heavy in the pause to follow. "I look forward to seeing her."

"Very good. Very good. You've been spending a great deal of time in her company of late, much to our delight."

"Yes," he echoed, feeling like a parrot.

Of course he spent a great deal of time with Lady Elise. He had no choice. Every time he turned around, the duchess was inviting her to dinner, or to their theater box, or for tea or a ride through the park. He could not escape the lass.

It was clear that the Birchwoods wanted him to spend time with her much as their son had done.

The duke leaned forward and tugged Con closer simultaneously, almost bringing their heads into contact. Con was not certain the reason for the closeness. No one else was in the room to overhear them.

"She's a lovely chit. Easy to like." The duke's eyes gleamed. "To say nothing of her pedigree. The Drafford title goes back as far as the Conqueror."

Con nodded slowly. "Yes, Your Grace."

Really, what else could he say?

"A feast for the eyes, too," Birchwood added. "Such beauty."

Con eased back a step, no longer able to endure the duke's less than fragrant breath in such close proximity. The man had a penchant for cigars and pickled pollock for breakfast. "Indeed."

The duke frowned at him. "You're not a very demonstrative fellow. Been that way ever since you were a lad. Such a stoic little lad when you were dropped off with us."

Days after his parents' deaths? Yes. Stoic could apply.

"I thought you would have grown out of that," the duke continued. "Reticence is not an admirable trait when courting a lady. A lady likes grand gestures." Birchwood fluttered a hand in the air. "They like to be wooed . . . for a beau to make grand proclamations." His fluttering hand curled into a fist as though he were seizing hold of something. "You have to be bold. Adventurous."

Of course, he could not help but consider the irony in this. He wondered if this was the same advice Birchwood had given his youngest son, Malcolm, who died from a broken neck when he fell from the trellis he was scaling to reach the bedchamber of his latest paramour, the very beautiful—*very married*—Lady Feckingham.

He refrained from asking, knowing Birchwood would not appreciate the reminder. The only thing more painful than the loss of his sons was the completely pointless way in which they had died. A splinter, a broken neck and choking. If it wasn't so tragic, it would be laughable.

Birchwood continued, "A man in love is a man of action."

Constantine resisted pointing out that he was *not* a man in love.

His cousin Winston had been in love. Specifically, he had been in love with the Lady Elise. At least, by all accounts. Everyone had been telling him that since almost the moment he had arrived in London. Winston had doted on his bride-to-be. It might have been a match arranged by their families, but his cousin had heartily been in favor of it.

It seemed since he was to fill his cousin's shoes, everyone thought he, too, should take on his cousin's betrothed . . . and display all the necessary infatuation with a woman he found agreeable and yet for whom he felt nothing. Only polite apathy.

He supposed it was a sound solution, as long as the girl was agreeable. He could do no better than Lady Elise. He had no misapprehensions when it came to that. She was far better than he. His superior in every way. Which was why he already knew what he would do. If the lass would have him, he would take her to wife.

It was the honorable thing to do. Lady Elise had planned on marrying the next Duke of Birchwood, after all, and he was now that man.

Old Birchwood's gaze looked off in the distance. "What month is . . ." His voice faded away as the answer came to him on his own. "Ah. Yes. They would have married by now. Dear Winston and Lady Elise."

A whimsical smile brushed the duke's lips as he nodded. "Perhaps I would have been looking forward to the arrival of my first grandchild by now, hm?"

An awkward silence fell.

The duke shook off his musings and his gaze sharpened, fixing on Constantine again. "You need to cease your dawdling. Life is short. No one knows that better than I do. Get married and get your heir secured." His lips twisted. "And then work on the next one. There is no such thing as security, no guarantees, but you can shore up your resources. The more offspring the better."

Constantine shifted his weight uneasily on his feet. It felt too soon to propose. Certainly more time was required than the few months he had been acquainted with Lady Elise. Winston had died scarcely a year ago. He knew the Birchwoods were anxious to see their line secured. They wanted him married and a child en route . . . but this was rash even for them. There were standards of mourning to be considered. The black crepe might have been removed a month ago, but it still felt hasty.

And yet Birchwood was an exalted peer. He had the ear of the queen. If anyone frowned on his actions, they would keep all opinions to themselves. In fact, crusty old peers of Birchwood's ilk were likely urging him to get Constantine hitched posthaste.

Lady Elise was an amenable young lady, but he sensed a certain reserve in her. He was not convinced she was receptive to his suit. For all the time they had spent in each other's company, she still felt like a stranger to him.

He rather thought it might always be that way. Were he to marry her, he would wake up in twenty years and still know her no better than he did now. They would be kind, dispassionate partners living together and yet detached from one another.

Not like Nora Langley. *Dispassionate* could never be a word applied to her. He'd been in her company only a few occasions, and he felt as though they had many more encounters between them. That was probably a result of uncovering her deceit. Once someone was revealed to be a devious fraud, were there really any barriers left?

"Do you know who stands to inherit following you? If you do not bring forth issue? Do you?" Birchwood demanded, his eyes looking a little wild. "Who is next in line after you?"

Con shook his head, alarmed at the directness of Birchwood's questioning, to say nothing of his agitation. Such forthrightness was so very uncharacteristic, so *very un*aristocratic of him, and Birchwood was every inch the blue-blooded noble.

"My solicitors are not definite, but they believe

they tracked the next in line to Argentina. They've sent an agent to ferret out some distant relation who settled in Buenos Aires over fifty years ago to see if he's still alive or has any issue on the off chance you should not come up to scratch. Can you imagine?" he sputtered. "I did my duty and now my legacy is left in such doubt."

Constantine cleared his throat uneasily, feeling the burden of responsibility so keenly. He did not know they had sent an agent to Argentina. "You may rest easy, Your Grace. There is no doubt," he promised. "I'll do my duty."

Birchwood peered at him long and hard before reaching for his arm and giving it another squeeze. "Don't fail me, lad. I've had too much disappointment in my life. Far too much. I don't need to see all of this"—his gaze lifted to the ceiling and surrounding room—"go to a stranger." He released a heavy sigh, his shoulders slumping a bit. "And unless I want to endure my dear wife's disappointment tonight, I'd best get dressed for dinner."

"Quite so." Con nodded, glad for the end to the awkward conversation.

Together they departed the office and made their way to their separate rooms.

Chapter 11

$\mathcal{N}$ora had to admit it. Bea knew what she was about when it came to dressing a lady.

Nora's hair had never looked so fine as it did now, piled atop her head in loose waves with two fat ringlets falling to drape over her bare shoulder. No wonder Bea had been so distressed to find herself Nora's maid. She'd been idle under Nora. It was a waste of her many talents.

She'd never worn the peach gown before so had not thought to protest when Bea chose to pack it—or chose to lay it out for this evening.

Now she knew she should have protested.

In fact, she should have better surveyed all the gowns Bea had selected for the trip. Naturally, she had pulled from the new wardrobe Nora acquired upon Marian marrying Warrington. They were all gorgeous clothes, much more fashionable than anything she ever wore. Nora ignored most of them, preferring her old familiar dresses.

Bea had packed none of those. Of course.

Staring at her reflection, she tugged at the bodice cutting into the swells of her breasts. "Is it possible that I've . . . grown since last fitted for this dress?"

Bea straightened from where she bent over, Nora's day dress in her arms. "Most definitely. That was well over a year ago."

Nora turned the scowl from her own reflection to Bea.

Bea pointed at each of her swelling breasts. "Those have definitely grown."

She shook her head. "I can't wear this!"

"You've nothing else to wear and it's perfectly appropriate. Fashions are a little more daring in Town. You're not going to raise any eyebrows."

She gripped her bodice with two hands and fought to tug the neckline higher, jumping lightly on the balls of her feet.

Bea swatted her hands away. "Stop that. You'll tear the fabric."

She worried if she bent over in the slightest she

might burst free. "This is unendurable," she muttered, trying to stuff the swelling flesh deeper inside her gown.

"Leave them alone and hurry now. You don't want to be late." Bea started tidying up the bedchamber. "Walk straight. No hunkering over."

Nora doubted she could manage that, but she would try. She was usually a confident individual who walked with her shoulders pulled back and her chest thrust out, her stride purposeful because she always knew her direction and what she was about.

But walking with her chest thrust out simply felt too dangerous. To do so, she risked exposing herself, and she was already a little out of her depth tonight. Dinner parties weren't her strong suit. It wouldn't do to bare herself in front of London's finest.

She left Bea tidying her chamber and departed the room, soaking in Bea's words, letting them fortify her as, alone in the corridor, she took a moment to lean back against her bedchamber door. *The gown is not daring by London standards. The gown is not daring by London standards.*

She pressed her palms flat against the door, using the time to gather her composure for the dinner that loomed ahead and reminding herself that she did far more difficult or unpleasant things all the time. It could not be any worse than excising a boil or drawing an infection out from a toenail.

"Miss Langley?"

Her head snapped up, her gaze searching the length of the corridor and landing on Sinclair.

"Good eve, Mr. Sinclair." She lifted away from her bedchamber door, smoothing her hands down the front of her skirts.

He approached at a sedate pace, his tread muffled on the runner.

Her nerves crackled to life as she faced his advance, his clean masculine scent drifting closer. She had already acknowledged to herself that he was handsome. In a dark, brooding kind of way. He looked especially fine tonight, however, in his black evening attire.

"Going down to dinner?" he inquired. His voice was all politeness, but his gaze was far from well-mannered as it roamed over her.

She resisted covering the exposed flesh of her chest with her hand. *The gown is not daring by London standards.*

She took Bea's words, wrapped herself in them and hoped they would console her in this most embarrassing moment, in her height of discomfort. What she wouldn't do for one of her well-worn, modest and comfortable wool gowns now.

Certainly, that would be its own form of awkwardness—her dining with the most elegant and refined nobility in a brown sack of a dress—but she might actually prefer that to *this*. To a stare that was decidedly *un*lascivious.

Although lascivious looks were not his style. She already knew that much of him. He was much too rigid, much too impassive. The army must have bled the emotion from him. Or perhaps he was simply born to be detached and immune to females. Or at least to *her*.

Perhaps there were other females he would react to with emotion.

Ladies whom he would not look at in distaste when they wore a risqué gown.

That was a rather lowering thought. She almost preferred for him to look at her with a lascivious leer instead of the way he looked at her now—as though she were something he stepped on and squashed beneath his shoe.

His gaze made its way back to her face.

Perhaps she was being overly sensitive. He'd surveyed her from head to toe in a matter of seconds. It was impossible to know what he was thinking.

"Ah. Yes, I am," she said.

He stopped before her and offered his arm. "Shall I escort you?"

She hesitated before taking hold of his proffered arm.

Beside him, she looked up and yet did not move. Not quite yet. It felt necessary to speak first—to say what needed to be said . . . what she felt compelled to say.

"Thank you."

An expression of gratitude was overdue.

He angled his head. "What are you thanking me for, Miss Langley?"

She moistened her lips. "For what you did, what you said to the duke." She flexed her fingers over his sleeve. "I wouldn't be here if not for you. Thank you for inviting me."

"Ah." He nodded. "Well, it was rather unexpected, I must confess. Until the words escaped my mouth, I did not know I would say them."

"Then why did you?"

Why did you lie for me?

He looked at her as though that answer were the most obvious thing in the world. "You said you could help the duchess. I'd be foolish not to give you that chance. For her sake, if nothing else."

For her sake. Of course. It wasn't because of

Nora. It was not because Nora asked him to do it. She was naught but an unwanted factor in all of this. She was here only for the duchess.

"Yes," she said in a little puff of breath. "Well, thank you. I'm here because of you."

"You're here because you barged your way in." His lips twisted in a semblance of a smile as they started down the corridor.

"Well. I needed your endorsement." She shrugged. "You gave it."

"No thanks needed. Help the duchess. That is all that is required."

Required. No pressure with that.

They proceeded down the corridor. "I spent most of the day with the duchess. She did not exhibit any symptoms. Presently, she seems in fine health."

"Give it some time. I've been told she has been afflicted for well over a year now with this malaise. As much as I wish her suffering would simply stop, I doubt it will."

"I will be patient then." Although patience wasn't her strong suit. She did not sit idle during her days. She certainly did not spend her days working on her needlepoint or as a companion to ladies of mature years. But that's what she would be doing as she waited for the duchess to get sick again.

"I'm sure she appreciates your company. She is accustomed to a vigorous social life. That has changed since she lost her sons and since the onset of this infirmity."

They descended the stairs.

"Has anyone thought whether her affliction has to do with the grief of losing her sons?"

"Possible, I suppose. I did wonder, but the timing does not seem significant. Her pains started before the death of her sons, after all. And when her grief was the most intense after losing Winston she was not afflicted during that time at all."

Her grief did not appear to be a trigger for her condition then.

They stopped before the drawing room doors. "Ready?"

She turned to face him. "It's just a dinner party," she said as though she attended dinner parties with nobles all the time and not just with her sisters and Warrington, the world's most *un*-noble noble. She had never felt any pressure or anxiety in Warrington's company.

This dinner, she suspected, would be different.

She would be dining with a duke and a duchess who fully acted the part. At least her day with the duchess had made her more comfortable in that august lady's company. The duke was another story. She had scarcely spent any time with him, but she did not think he took her very seriously. Actually, she doubted that he took her any way at all. He was a man at the top of his world. She was merely a female, and not one of particular note as she was without rank or wealth or name or great beauty.

She knew from Bea, who had proven herself to be quite the fount of information, that Lady Elise would be in the company of her aunt, the Dowager Marchioness of Cheswick. The other guests would be the duke and duchess's dear friends, the Baron and Baroness Loftin.

It was a strange thing to consider that she would be the only one at the table who was of humble origins. Even Sinclair. He might be a *mister* right now, but he was the Birchwood heir. That was his destiny. No one would ever look at him or treat him as a plain *mister* again. He was more, *better* as far as the rest of the world was concerned.

He held the door for her and waved her within to the "just a dinner party" that waited.

Chapter 12

*L*ady Elise was as lovely as purported to be. The Birchwood staff had not exaggerated that fact to Bea.

Apparently rank and wealth were not blessings enough. Beauty had been bestowed upon her as well. Halfway through dinner it was further established—she was as kind as she was charming. No human should be so blessed.

Sinclair sat taciturn, replying when spoken to, but rarely engaging in the conversation . . . and certainly not to the lively degree of Lady Elise. Nora acknowledged they would be well matched. Lady Elise would make up for his reserve with her vivacious spirit.

The young woman engaged Nora in conversation, inquiring after Nora's interest in what she called "the herbal arts." She did not even look bored as Nora explained to her the various uses rosemary served that had nothing to do with food.

"I envy you your talent, Miss Langley," Lady Elise announced as she delicately angled her spoon into her soup bowl.

"Do you?" The dowager marchioness looked mildly affronted.

"Yes," Lady Elise replied evenly. "I do."

"I was fortunate to have an excellent teacher in my father," she replied.

"Ah. Well, there you have it. My father, God rest his soul, was only ever very talented at cards and drink."

"Elise!" her aunt exclaimed in disapproval.

"Oh, please, Aunt." Lady Elise rolled her eyes. "Everyone knows it."

"Yes, well, perhaps, but you needn't talk about it so openly." She glanced at Nora with a flare of her nostrils, as though she were responsible for Lady Elise's forthrightness. "Especially in mixed company."

Mixed company? Meaning Nora, the peasant in their midst. She fought to maintain a neutral expression in the face of the woman's sly contempt for her.

Lady Elise shook her head in dismissal of her aunt and focused on Nora again. "Have you considered extending your education so that you might practice more formally?"

"In what way?"

"Why, becoming a doctor yourself," she said as though that were most obvious—or a simple thing to do.

Nora studied her for a moment, trying to decipher if her question originated from a place of ignorance. Perhaps she truly did not realize the feat of that task. Or perhaps she thought Nora was up for such a monumental task? "Medical schools in Britain refuse admittance to females."

"Absurd," Lady Elise exclaimed, her cheeks pink with outrage. Evidently she had not been aware of this imbalance.

Nora could not help but like the woman even more.

"Is it?" the duke inquired mildly as he lifted his glass and took a long sip of wine. "Anatomy and physiology hardly seem appropriate areas of studies for a lady."

"Hear, hear," the dowager marchioness seconded. "A refined lady would not sully herself in the field of medicine. How could one even entertain such a notion?" She sent a reproving look to her niece. "Ladies must protect their sensibilities and shroud themselves in the proper trappings of virtuous womanhood." Her stare turned then and fell rather pointedly on Nora.

"Indeed. Virtuous womanhood must be protected," the baron parroted as he stuffed his mouth full of meat, his crooked yellow teeth chomping down on the mint-dressed lamb. Juice dribbled down his chin as he chewed. He lifted his napkin to half-heartedly mop up the mess. He didn't catch it all and brown spots soon appeared on his dress shirt and brocade waistcoat.

Nora cringed at the unattractive sight, wondering who would *protect* the world from the sight of the baron eating his dinner.

For some reason she felt compelled to look at Sinclair, to see if he appeared to share their opinions on the role of women in medicine.

She assumed he was like-minded given his reaction at discovering she was the true author of her father's letters. He claimed his outrage was due to her deceit, but she wondered if it was truly over discovering she was a female dispensing medical advice. She suspected he was not broad-minded when it came to women occupying nontraditional roles, and for some reason she felt a keen sense of disappointment in him, which she had no right to feel. He was not family nor friend nor anyone for whom she should feel disappointment.

He stared back at her, his face void of expression. And yet he offered no defense on her behalf and expressed no indignation.

"Poppycock," Lady Elise offered.

"What say you, Sinclair?" the duke called across the table.

Nora stared at him, waiting, expecting a decided lack of support.

"In the army I observed grisly injuries that I shall not recount here." He paused, a muscle flickering along his jaw as though caught up in a particular unfortunate memory. She tried not to let that sight of vulnerability within him affect her. She did not want to soften toward him when he so obviously was about to disparage the role of women in medicine. He then resumed speaking. "Innumerable injuries. Some fatal. I stood witness during many a surgery that would unquestionably offend those of delicate constitutions."

"See there now." The dowager marchioness bobbed her head in satisfaction. "Delicate constitutions must be shielded."

Nora inhaled, her fingers tightening around her cutlery. "And yet women," she began with a bit of heat, "are allowed to be nurses . . . to wipe snot and cleanse wounds and change bedpans. To say nothing of the rigors and dangers of childbirth we are expected to endure. There is nothing delicate in that activity, which, of course, is deemed appropriate lest mankind cease to exist."

A dead silence met her proclamation. All eyes fixed on her as though she had spouted a second head. Someone dropped their cutlery and it clattered loudly against a plate, shattering the uneasy hush.

Lady Elise looked vastly entertained as she glanced up and down the table at every face, ostensibly to gauge their reaction to Nora's tirade.

And it was a tirade. Nora could hear either one of her sisters' voices in her ear, telling her she had overstepped. Too late now though.

Sinclair cleared his throat and announced, "I was not finished."

She settled her glare back on him, braced and ready for more doubtlessly disappointing words.

"Delicate constitutions are not reserved to one gender."

"That's true. My sweet Malcolm could never stand the sight of blood. Poor lad. He would swoon at the sight of it." The duchess cut a delicate piece of lamb and placed it in her mouth, chewing neatly.

"Precisely. As to the matter of who is best suited to work in medicine, I say it depends on the individual and gender has nothing to do with it."

The table, again, fell to silence.

He'd surprised her. She did not know how to respond. She felt her mouth open and close several times.

Lady Elise smiled at her and then turned her full attention on to Sinclair, as though he were suddenly worth noticing. "Well said, Mr. Sinclair."

Lady Elise fiddled with her spoon, turning it over in her chilled soup as she gazed at Sinclair, her expression almost . . . besotted. There were no other words for her suddenly starry-eyed expression. She angled her head, arching her long, elegant neck. Her slim fingers stroked the tender line of her throat, almost as though calling attention there.

Again, Nora was confronted with the fact that there was much of her to admire. Her luminescent skin only highlighted the lush beauty of her chestnut hair and hazel eyes.

Lady Elise had not looked at him once during the entire evening, but now she appeared quite enraptured of him.

It was almost as though in coming to Nora's defense, he had esteemed himself in her eyes.

Splendid.

Nora lifted her glass and took a deep drink, trying to fight the strange swell of emotions in her chest. She filtered through them, singling them out one at a time and setting them aside for examination.

Annoyance. Resentment. Oh, and one emotion that felt dangerously close to . . . inadequacy, and she hated that. It wasn't like her. Nora Langley was not one to ever suffer feelings of inadequacy. In order to do that, she'd have to care what others thought and the opinions of others had never ranked as a very high priority in her life.

Even though Bea had done wonders to make her look her best, she felt like a dull bird sitting a few seats down from Lady Elise, who seemed to know how to tilt her head and place her hand on her neck just so, in a way that made Nora feel flushed and faintly naughty . . . like she was spying on a couple sneaking a kiss.

Lady Elise spoke again, still brushing a hand along her neck, over her pulse point in that flirty way.

"That's a very fair point, Mr. Sinclair. Why shouldn't a woman be permitted a medical license? Goodness knows whenever I've fallen ill, it's always been a woman to take care of me."

"Elise," the dowager marchioness intervened in a reprimanding tone, and Nora suspected she used that tone often on her niece. "Don't encourage such nonsense. Miss Langley doubtlessly wants to start a household of her own soon. She will not continue her work as an . . . *herbalist* into the future." Lady Elise's aunt uttered *herbalist* as though it were a dirty word.

"Not everyone's vocation is marriage, Aunt," Lady Elise said sharply. Perhaps too sharply? A quick glance revealed that the Duke and Duchess of Birchwood both looked perturbed at that announcement from the woman they clearly hoped to be their future daughter-in-law.

"Rubbish. Every young woman is after marriage." The baroness tittered. "Trust me." She waved her spoon in a small circle. "We had three daughters and they could scarcely wait to leave our house to start households of their own."

Nora lifted her napkin to her lips to stifle a laugh as it occurred to her that these daughters may have been in a rush to marry simply to escape their parents.

Lowering her napkin, she declared very soberly, "I can assure you I am not in a hurry to start my own household. But then I suppose I'm an anomaly in that regard."

"Anomaly indeed." Somehow the dowager marchioness managed to take a sip from her glass through pinched lips. Impressive.

"Nonsense," the baron intervened. "Only the ineligible females profess no desire to wed."

Nora stiffened, but fixed a smile to her face,

pretending *not* to be offended at being character-ized as ineligible.

"Your sister is married to the Duke of War-rington, is she not, Miss Langley?" the dowager marchioness asked.

"Yes." Nora nodded, glad for the change of subject. She was quite done discussing the valid-ity of women practicing medicine.

"Was there not some notoriety surrounding him?" She looked contemplative as she posed the question. "He never comes to Town."

"Town life is not for everyone," the Duchess of Birchwood chimed in.

"Yes, but does he not neglect his duties in the House?" The lady shook her head in disapproval. "Some people have no sense of duty."

"My brother-in-law happens to prefer country life," Nora explained, trying to keep the defen-siveness from her voice. "And he's quite besotted with my sister, his wife, and she, too, happens to prefer life in Brambledon." Nora shrugged as if the matter were as simple as that.

"How singular." The dowager marchioness shook her head, visibly scoffing, clearly not thinking it romantic or acceptable in any way.

"This Brambledon sounds as though it begs a visit," the duchess put forth with a kind smile for Nora. "It sounds positively charming."

"Well, I am so glad *you* don't eschew Town or we would never have the pleasure of your company," Lady Elise said, ever so gracious as she stared directly at Nora.

It really was unfortunate. For some reason, Nora wanted to dislike her.

Yes, it was poorly done of her, but there it was. Lady Elise was lovely and would make a lovely duchess, a lovely wife to Sinclair. As far as Nora could tell, she was far better than he deserved and he should waste no time legitimizing the match.

"Yes. How long will you stay?" The question was polite and innocent enough, but there was something in the dowager marchioness's eyes that felt . . . unkind. Unlike her niece, the lady did not like her and seemed to want Nora gone from here.

"Well. I . . . er, I have no set departure date yet." She was not about to disclose the reason she was here was to help the duchess, and as she had not accomplished anything on that score she was not leaving anytime soon.

"With your particular talents, I'm certain they are missing you, m'dear. I'm assuming you treat Warrington's tenants? And the villagers?"

Nora nodded.

The dowager marchioness continued, "Well. Don't tarry here too long when you're needed at home."

"Thank you for your concern." She lifted her glass in salute to the lady and then took a long sip, perfectly aware the woman cared nothing for the health and well-being of tenant farmers.

Over the rim of her glass, she saw Sinclair watching her. He'd been far from gregarious this evening other than that brief unexpected rise to her defense.

They all adjourned to the drawing room after dinner.

Sinclair and Lady Elise paired off for a game of cards. It was clear the game was to be exclusive between them. They sat at a small marble-topped table that seated only two.

The dowager marchioness drifted toward her in her black bombazine, her starched skirts cracking like brittle twigs as she hovered over Nora like a great bird of prey. "They're a handsome pair, are they not?"

Nora smiled tightly. "Indeed, they are."

"We were crushed, of course, at the passing of Winston. It was so sudden, and so tragic after losing Malcolm and Albert. Too bad you were not here then." The dowager marchioness clucked her tongue. While the sound clearly intended to be sympathetic it only came across as scathing and mocking. "Perhaps your vast skills could have done something to save him."

Nora might not be the most adept at navigating social circles and people, but she felt certain the woman was patronizing her.

Of course, Nora could not react. She had to shove down her ire and be polite and make idle chitchat. "Were Lady Elise and Lord Birchwood betrothed for very long?"

"Oh, they knew each other all of their lives. It was always expected they would marry, but they only officially became engaged a few months prior to Winston's death."

"How very sad."

"Indeed, indeed. Elise has trained all her life for this. We always thought she would be the next Duchess of Birchwood. It is only right that Mr. Sinclair upholds the honor of his family and does right by offering for my niece."

"Oh." Nora was not certain what she was expected to say to that. For that matter, she was not even certain why Lady Elise's aunt was singling her out for this conversation. And Nora did feel singled out. "Mr. Sinclair is an honorable man."

"Yes," she commented mildly, tipping her head and studying Nora thoughtfully. "He is. Interesting how you know him so well already."

"It only takes a short time in Mr. Sinclair's company to discern his character."

"Speaking of durations of time . . . should your

visit here not be coming to an end, m'dear? I know you said you did not know yet when you would depart, but I hope it is sooner rather than later." She lowered her voice to a hush. "Perhaps I'm bold saying this, but the duke and duchess may be entertaining again and this house no longer shrouded in mourning, but it is very much a place of grief. Their loss is great. As you're from the country and rather provincial, I fear you may lack direction in such matters. You should not overstay your welcome, m'dear. Besides, I am quite certain your little country hamlet misses you. Won't you be more comfortable there? Where you belong? Certainly you must feel a little out of sorts here."

Leave. Go. Be gone. Take yourself back to the den from whence you came.

Those were the words she heard. Her first London dinner party and one of the guests wanted to make sure she understood that she didn't belong here.

"Thank you for the advice. I will keep that in mind." She smoothed a hand over her skirts and noted that it trembled ever so slightly. "You know, I suddenly feel weary. If you will pardon me, I'm going to retire for the night."

"Of course." The dowager marchioness smiled smugly, looking supremely pleased with herself.

Nora quickly rose to her feet and bid good eve to everyone, primarily focusing on her hosts, her attention straying only briefly to the others. Especially to Sinclair. For some reason, she found it difficult to look at him with the dowager's words ringing in her ears. *Certainly you must feel a little out of sorts here.*

The woman was right. She was out of sorts and everyone knew it. Even Sinclair. Perhaps that was the true reason he had not wanted her here. Nora did not belong here, and he knew it.

Chapter 13

Constantine looked up from the ledger he was perusing with a sigh and rubbed at the back of his neck where tension seemed to be gathering.

Since that miserable dinner a few days ago, he continued to bury himself in the task of familiarizing himself with the Birchwood estate. The duke and duchess might spend all their time in Town, but they were in possession of several properties throughout the country that required managing.

He knew his self-imposed solitude couldn't last. He was courting Lady Elise and he knew what was expected of him. *Courting*. He needed to call on her lest she think his interest had waned.

He had promised as much to old Birchwood.

He knew they expected him to propose soon. Despite that, he had kept to himself for three days.

He dined out at his club or took a tray in his room. No one had remarked on his absence yet, but he knew it was coming. They would think he was avoiding people and they would be right.

He had to face that this was the reality of his life. The duke had made that reality perfectly clear, after all. This kind of delay would not be tolerated, and truthfully it was cowardly. Even by Constantine's standards. He could not hide from the people in his life forever. Of course, of all the people he was avoiding, he could think only of her. Nora.

He had to face *her*—for however long she was here.

Seated at the office's great mahogany desk, he stared out the window that looked out over the back garden.

As though his thoughts had conjured her, she suddenly appeared.

Nora strolled arm in arm with the duchess amid the wild profusion of flowers. The sunlight turned her hair to spun gold. He could stare at it all day long.

Immediately, he felt the tug of a smile on his mouth. She had discomfited everyone at dinner the other night with her bold speech and ideas.

Except for Lady Elise, who found her to be a delightful bluestocking. Elise was forward thinking that way—a definite point in her favor.

Everyone else had looked at Nora as though she were a two-headed creature in their midst. She knew she was a bit of a bluestocking. Very well. A very *significant* bluestocking.

He chuckled and fell back in his chair. She had been the single delight of an otherwise miserable evening, which was troubling. Everyone else at the table happened to be his peers, the manner of people with whom he would spend the rest of his life. She would not be in his life. Not permanently. He should not enjoy her so much.

Nora Langley did not possess an inauthentic bone in her body, which was strange considering he knew her to be a proven deceiver.

The duchess pointed at a flower and Nora crouched down to collect it for her.

He watched, riveted as she tucked the flower behind the older lady's ear. The duchess had not suffered a spell since Nora arrived.

He hated to think it, but he almost wished she was hurting so that Nora could attend to her, fix her and then be on her way, every tempting inch of her on her way back to her precious Brambledon.

Tempting.

God, no. He could not think about her in such

terms. Just as he should not think of her in that dress from the other night.

Certainly she had looked as no country miss should look in that gown. She was young. He had thought that when he first met her. A young girl with no life experiences beyond that of her small village—someone who played at writing letters and signing her dead papa's name to them.

He had at least a decade on her and he had not expected to feel a sharp stab of desire for her when he stumbled on her in the hall outside her bedchamber, looking like a luscious peach. Certainly, she was much too young for him. Except in that dress, she had looked ripe and ready. His teeth had ached looking at her. He'd longed for a taste.

The ladies turned and headed back to the house. Presumably, their stroll was over. His attempt to get any work accomplished was over, too.

"Blast it," he muttered, pushing from the desk.

Nora had been stuck here since her arrival, playing companion to the duchess. She was probably feeling a bit hemmed in, too.

He found her and the duchess in the drawing room, a tea service between them. One of the maids was arranging a small plate of cakes and biscuits for the duchess.

"Ah, Constantine, come and join us," the duchess greeted as her gaze alighted on him.

She waved him over with an imperious hand. "We've not seen much of you. You've been working much too hard. It's not healthy, you know."

He sank down on a wingback chair across from them. "There is much I need to learn."

"Well, you've always been a clever lad. I'm sure it won't pose any difficulty for you. Don't you agree, Nora?"

Nora blinked. "I did not know Mr. Sinclair as a lad, but I agree. He appears intelligent."

Appears. She was comical.

The duchess nodded happily as she bit into a cake, oblivious to Nora's mocking of him. "What plans have you, Mr. Sinclair?"

"I was thinking of a visit to Middlesex Hospital—"

"Oh. Indeed?" Nora's entire body leaned forward in her seat, an eager light filling her eyes.

"Oh, dear." The duchess frowned over the teacup she was lifting to her lips. "Is something amiss with you, too?"

"Me? Oh, no. I am quite hale. The hospital has dissecting rooms and surgical theaters." Nora's eyes were now as round as saucers, watching him as though he were announcing words that signified life and death for her. It was deliberate, of course. He knew what he was doing.

She really was the most peculiar female. Other

girls cared about shopping and gossip. Especially girls with means, and as the sister-in-law of the Duke of Warrington, she had the means to be as spoiled and vain as any debutante.

Except she wasn't. She chose not to be. Instead, she was someone who became glassy-eyed with excitement at the mention of visiting a hospital.

"Surgical theaters? My, that sounds impressive," the duchess said as she selected another biscuit.

"I thought Miss Langley might like to visit and observe them with me."

"Oh, yes. Yes, yes, yes." Nora nodded wildly, rising from the sofa, mindless of the small plate on her lap. It slid to the floor, the biscuits and cakes tumbling onto the rug.

"Oh!" Nora dropped to the floor and hastily picked up the food.

He could not help feeling a happy swelling in his chest. He had suspected this would interest her, but to see her this overjoyed and over such a small thing . . . well, he felt so gratified.

The duchess giggled. "I think you can take that as assent. She would like to accompany you, my good sir."

Nora rose hurriedly to her feet, fairly bouncing in place. "When? Now? Today? When shall we go?"

"Yes. I was thinking today. Mortimer Street isn't too far a carriage ride." He glanced at the duchess. "Unless you are needed here?"

The duchess waved at them. "I have no need of either one of you. Go, go. Enjoy yourselves. Be young and merry whilst you can."

Nora glanced down at her gown. "Give me a moment to change and I will meet you right back here." She pointed to the floor as though it were imperative he understand where they should meet.

"Very well—"

His words faded as he watched her whirl around and flee the room.

The duchess giggled again. "Well, you have made her the happiest of women."

He suppressed a smile. "It's only a small thing. No hardship."

"You are a good and generous man, Sinclair, to go out of your way and do such a thing for our Miss Langley," she praised. "I'm certain you can't be interested in touring a hospital. Not when you could be spending your time with lovely Elise."

"Of course," he said tightly.

Spending an afternoon with Nora was no chore at all, but he had no wish to argue the point with the duchess for fear that she might suspect the truth—that spending time with Nora was something he actually longed to do, that he had orchestrated this outing because he wanted to. For himself.

Indeed it was no hardship at all—not in the way the duchess made it sound, but he could not rightly protest to that. Not without making it appear he did not want to spend time with Lady Elise. Lady Elise, the very woman with whom he *ought* to be spending time. After his conversation with the duke, that much was abundantly understood. At least he'd agreed to that.

The notion for this outing with Nora had come to him rather suddenly when he spotted her strolling the gardens with the Duchess of Birchwood. He had been seized with the spontaneous impulse to invite her on an excursion to Middlesex Hospital, of all places. He knew she would want to go as it was the site of a medical school, and they offered tours to the public.

Some ladies longed for a trip to Bond Street, but Nora Langley was not like most ladies. She was not like anyone he had ever met. He knew she would rather see an infirmary or visit a maternity floor or observe the surgical theater at Middlesex. He surmised that for her such a thing would be equitable to Christmas morning, and strangely, he felt compelled to give her that. He wanted to see her smile.

Chapter 14

$\mathcal{N}$ora emerged from the surgical theater alongside Mr. Sinclair, feeling a little dazed and lightheaded and breathless—but only in the best respect.

She fanned herself with her reticule. It was quite the most extraordinary spectacle she had ever seen. She and Sinclair had been allowed to sit in the theater and observe the removal of an appendix! It was quite the most marvelous day.

They'd sat on one of the top rows, above several medical students. There were more students on the ground floor observing, too. Nora assumed they were further along in their studies as they were granted such close access. All were men, of course. Other than a few sidelong glances, no one had paid her presence much attention, too riveted upon the surgery being performed.

"That was extraordinary. Can you imagine cutting into someone and holding his life in your hands?" She cupped her hands before her and flexed her fingers as though she were holding an actual human organ, as though she herself possessed the talent and skill to save a life.

"No, I cannot imagine doing that myself." He smiled mildly as he strolled alongside her.

She took several deep breaths to regain her composure and temper her excitement. He must think her overly stimulated and provincial.

Nora had cut into flesh before, but nothing like what she had witnessed today. Even as her father's assistant, she had never seen him perform anything like that. "It was all terribly exciting."

Mr. Sinclair lifted one shoulder. "I have seen enough blood to last a lifetime."

"Yes, I can understand that, but this day's bloodshed did not signify loss of life. That surgery saved a life and perhaps more than one life through the gaining of experience by all those who watched."

"Perhaps," he allowed.

A rueful smile curled her lips as she stared at

him. He did not fool her in the least. He had been fascinated, too.

"Admit it, Mr. Sinclair," she charged, arching an eyebrow in challenge. "You were as riveted as I was."

"I'll allow it was not *uninteresting*. I've seen army surgeons at work before but never have I observed anything like that . . . never anything with such, such . . ."

"Precision," she supplied.

"Yes," he agreed with a nod as they continued down the gallery, side by side.

"My father would have appreciated this today." Likely Papa had seen such a surgery performed before when he himself attended medical school, but it would have been quite the special thing for the two of them to have observed something like this together. "He would have . . ." She paused, gathering her thoughts, feeling her composure slip as she thought of her dearest Papa. "He would have loved it. Thank you." She stopped and he stopped in kind. She turned to face him. "Thank you for thinking to bring me here," she said haltingly, feeling a little awkward with her surge of emotion.

He looked equally uncomfortable, as though he didn't know what to do with her gratitude.

"You have no business here!" The words cracked like a whip over the air.

Tensing, she stopped and turned, searching for the source of the angry voice.

Her gaze swept the length of the gallery. A man with a shiny-knobbed cane approached with very sharp steps, a sneer twisting his lips. His eyes flashed back and forth between Nora and Sinclair in a fiery display of ire for which she could not account.

Astonishment rippled through her to find herself the target of this stranger's glare. She should not have felt such sentiment. Virulent men came as no shock. She well knew they existed in the world. In truth, they abounded.

A couple years ago, Marian had been abducted by a man who thought his rights superseded her own. For all the good men that existed, there were always some who were content only when crushing a female beneath his boot.

She braced herself, knowing more was to come from this particular gentleman. Indeed, the red mottling of his face warned her that he was just getting started.

"*Females,*" he began, dropping the word as though it alone was something objectionable, "do not belong here." He lifted his cane and shook the gleaming head in her direction.

Sinclair went as rigid as a board beside her. His arm beneath her fingers bunched and tightened and he took a step forward, clearly ready to intercede on her behalf, but she tugged him back with a swift shake of her head. She did not require a protector, and she did not need a public disaster. Neither one of them needed that spectacle.

The stranger stopped directly before them. The man was broad of frame and nearly as tall as Sinclair. She resisted the urge to shrink back. She was accustomed to judgmental stares, but no one, especially no *stranger*, had ever confronted her so very openly or aggressively.

Even after Papa's death, when her family was at their poorest, she had been accorded civility from her fellow residents of Brambledon.

Still keeping a tight grip on Sinclair's arm, she forced herself to square her shoulders and stand tall in the face of his glower. She had no reason to be frightened, after all. "I have just as much right to be here as you, sir."

His face, if possible, reddened further and she realized *she* had shocked *him*. He did not expect her to challenge him. Evidently he was not accustomed to such oppositional behavior from females. She was serving up all manner of surprises to this man today.

His mouth opened and closed before he spit out, "Impertinent chit!"

A low growl sounded from the vicinity of Sinclair beside her. She gave his arm a reassuring squeeze. She sensed as much as she observed passersby stopping to gawk at them and the spectacle they were creating. She needed to do her best to keep things from escalating even more.

"Why?" she asked in an even voice. "Because I dare to improve my mind?" If he could address her so rudely, then she could resort to bluntness, too. "What are you so afraid of? That women might gain the wisdom to rise up against men like you?"

One of the nearby gawkers pointed at them and she overheard a whispered, *"Birchwood."* Apparently people were accurately identifying and connecting Sinclair to Birchwood.

The man, still resembling an apoplectic fish, turned on Sinclair then. "Get your woman in hand, sirrah. She needs a tighter bridle."

Outrage flared through her, constricting her chest. She opened her mouth to unleash on him, but Sinclair beat her to it, replying in a mockingly genial voice, "She is not *my* woman, sir. She is her own person. And the last time I verified . . . wait, let me be certain." He stepped back from Nora and scrutinized her. Pinching his chin, he looked her up and down leisurely. "It appears she is no horse in need of bridling. She looks quite human to me."

Now the stranger's red face was more purple. Clearly he had expected some form of support from Sinclair.

The man's eyes narrowed and he pointed at Sinclair in a stabbing motion. "I know who you are."

"Do you?" Sinclair inquired, the corners of his mouth tightening, his only outward reaction to the statement. "I don't believe I've had the pleasure . . ."

"Oh. Yes, I know you. I'm a member of your club. Well, I should say, Birchwood's club. I saw you there with him not very long ago, trailing after his coattails."

At the mention of Birchwood, Sinclair tensed. She felt it ever so subtly as she stood beside him.

"Indeed?" Sinclair inquired. "I did not see you . . . and Birchwood did not see fit to introduce us." It was a subtle slight, but felt nonetheless. *Birchwood does not deem you important or he would have made introductions.* True or not, that was his insinuation.

The gentleman's gaze flicked to Nora. "Does he know you keep company with such . . . *radical* females?"

Radical? She sniffed and lifted one shoulder in a half shrug. It would not be the first time someone called her that. Even her own family had been known to call her that, although never with any real heat.

"Oh, this lady here, you mean?" He glanced at Nora. "She is a close family friend and a guest of the Duke and Duchess of Birchwood."

That left the man fumbling for words. "Wh—"

Sinclair nodded cheerfully and tipped his hat at the sputtering man. "Good day, sir."

With a hand on her elbow, he turned them both about and together they continued down the gallery.

She could not help herself. She giggled. "His expression was too perfect," she said.

She knew Sinclair would not agree with any of the vile man's objections. He had chosen to bring her here, after all. But she had not expected him to be quite so amusing in his defense of her.

At first, she had feared he would resort to fisticuffs to defend her honor. Violence was never the answer. It only beget more violence. Sinclair had done as she wished and refrained. Warmth fluttered in her chest because he had stayed his impulse . . . for her. When she put a hand on his arm he had held himself back.

He was a man of reserve and restraint. Rigid

control. A man who never lost his composure. He did not make jests or engage in levity. And yet he had used wit and humor to set that jackanapes in his place.

Sinclair shrugged. "I could have been serious with him, but he was ridiculous. He deserved ridiculousness in turn."

"I suspect he wanted you to paddle my bum as though I were a child in need of punishment." She was still giggling at her words when she sent him a glance.

Her giggle died swiftly in her throat when her gaze met his.

His dark eyes gleamed deeper and darker than they ever had before.

Heat crept up her face as she envisioned the scene she had just suggested: herself tossed over Sinclair's knee with her skirts hiked up . . . with his big hand on her bare bottom, making contact, touching, stroking her . . .

She tried to swallow, but her throat suddenly felt impossibly tight. The urge to fidget pumped though her . . . especially as his gaze continued its thorough examination of her, seeing too much. Seeing beyond the exterior. It felt like he was looking past everything, past skin and bones to the essence of her.

Certainly this *look* was different.

No man had ever taken measure of her in such a way before. No gentlemen in Brambledon, of course. Definitely not.

While not unattractive, she was not the beauty either one of her sisters were regarded to be.

She was the peculiar sister, the individual people called to attend their ague. No gentleman ever viewed her in a romantic fashion and she suspected that lancing festering boils might have something to do with that. And yet she had never cared enough to stop being who she was and change into someone else to be more likeable. She preferred being herself even if no gentleman liked her that way.

She snapped her gaze forward again, wondering at the strange look in his eyes.

Walking down the gallery with her hand on his arm, she could still feel those eyes of his trained on her—and something else. Something more. A subtle energy radiated from him, reaching her, enveloping her.

Why did I mention him spanking my bottom?

As the mortifying memory of that—and the vision of him actually doing so—ran over and over in her mind, the heat in her face intensified to scorching levels.

Certainly her words had not . . . titillated him?

The rigid former colonel was not that manner

of man. He did not surrender to base desires and wickedness. She had not—*did not*—affect him. He was much too upright for that.

The walk outside was a blur as her mind whirled and her face burned and her nostrils flared, full of the scent of him: soap, man and something else that was inherently him.

Somehow they reached the carriage and Sinclair assisted her up into the Birchwood family coach. He rapped on the ceiling and the conveyance gave a small lurch as they started for home. *Home?* Well, not her home.

Birchwood House was not her home.

When she was a little girl, she had played dress up in Marian's clothes, always wanting to be older, wanting to be like her big sister, pretending to be what she was not—a proper grown-up. The clothes had never fit, of course. They'd swallowed her, but still she had played. Still, she had pretended.

That was what Birchwood House felt like to her. Ill-fitting clothes.

She felt like an imposter beneath its roof. A little girl at a game of pretend. It was not natural. It would never be natural. Never be home.

It was Sinclair's home. Natural to him. It was where he belonged as someday it would all be his. *His and Lady Elise's.* A reminder that felt necessary for some reason.

Together, he and Lady Elise would reign over Birchwood House and all its haughty servants like rulers of a small kingdom.

That would be his life.

Hers would be somewhere else.

Chapter 15

$\mathcal{N}$ora tried not to look at him as the carriage progressed. The air between them felt a little different since they left the surgical theater. Overly warm, stifling, almost . . . charged.

She studied her hands in her lap, then the seat squabs, then the curtained windows. Everywhere and anywhere but at him. Only it was not that simple when he sat across from her in the carriage. It was *beyond* difficult *not* to look at him when he was directly in front of her. The temptation was too strong.

Because she looked. She could not stop herself.

Except he wasn't looking at her anymore, which should have been a relief, but it was oddly . . . disappointing.

Her regret was real, lodging in her heart. She studied him freely without that devouring look trained on her. No more dark and intense and smoldering eyes that she felt right down in her belly.

He was looking out the window, even though the curtains were mostly drawn. Only a small crack was left parted, allowing a trickle of light inside the confines.

Her shoulders slumped as she fell back against her seat, disappointed their excursion had come to an end.

They moved along slowly, the sounds of other carriages clattering outside their own saved them from total silence. The muffled sounds helped cover up the dead air inside the carriage.

Somewhat.

She was aware of the rustling of his clothes as he shifted his weight. The rasp of his breathing as he expelled air . . . as though he was beleaguered and grew weary of her company. That would be unsurprising. He probably regretted the outing and the public confrontation he had just suffered as a consequence.

Why would he not be weary of her? He was the heir to a dukedom. He was an important man now, and would only gain in prominence when he one day claimed his position as the Duke of

Birchwood. He was a busy man. For goodness' sake, he was courting a proper lady, the daughter of an earl, and learning dukely things.

He would not be a duke like her brother-in-law. She already knew that much. He would follow Birchwood's lead and spend his days in Town and take his seat in the House and live his life in a proper lordly fashion.

Obviously he did not appreciate the unfavorable attention she had brought down upon his head. She winced. His association with her would not earn him any approval among his peers. That much was clear. If the ugly scene with that vile gentleman did not prove that, then there was Birchwood's dinner party to remind her.

He'd been most attentive this day. Polite and cordial, but this—*she*—was not what he wanted. He'd been clear on that when she arrived.

She was only here as the Birchwood's guest in order to help him, or, specifically, to help the duchess, and so far she hadn't helped him with anything at all. She was of no service to him. No help at all. She was an inconvenience. The duchess seemed fine. Hale and hearty, in fact. She couldn't stay here forever on the chance the duchess became ill again.

Nora should go home where she belonged. She had a family and a life waiting for her . . . a purpose and vocation. She missed her laboratory and all her things. As much as members of the community called her eccentric, she knew she was needed there. She was wanted in Brambledon. She had a place there. Always. Not here. Never here.

As soon as she returned to Birchwood House, she would start planning her return home.

She gasped as their carriage ground to a halt, her hand flying to the loop swaying overhead to catch her balance.

Oh, rot. A delay was the last thing she wanted. When she inhaled deeply, she caught his scent again. Masculine with a faint whiff of soap.

She wanted to get back to the house, to her chamber and her privacy where she could pout in relative peace and safety. Away from him.

Awkwardness swelled around them as they sat planted, the moments dragging into minutes. She folded her hands over her lap and unfolded them. Then folded them again. Restless energy danced along her nerves.

Usually she did not feel so uncomfortable. A sense of awkwardness required self-awareness. *Usually* she was indifferent to how others perceived her.

At least she had never cared before.

She did not like these sudden . . . *feelings*. It

was not her way. She did not like caring what he thought about her. This sudden interest and concern for how Sinclair perceived her was vexing.

He leaned forward and the sudden movement made her flinch. Her hands flew to clench the edge of the velvet seat. Fingers curling. Knuckles tight.

He paused and looked at her, evidently aware of her reaction, and that brought a rush of heat to her face.

His gaze lingered on her a moment longer before he proceeded, scooting forward to part the curtains and peer outside their carriage for a better view of the traffic. His intent all along, apparently, was to look outside. Not to touch her. Of course not. He had always been circumspect toward her.

Except he was so close. His face inches away from her as he investigated the state of affairs outside. She could practically count his eyelashes—all dark and lush and long.

"Anything amiss?" she asked, hating how breathless she sounded.

"I cannot see if there's an accident or anything of the sort ahead. Hopefully we'll be moving along soon."

He dropped back down on the seat again with a sigh, but this time he seemed closer, his bigger body encroaching on her space in the tight confines. He stretched his long legs so that his feet settled alongside hers.

She smiled shakily. "It seems we are stuck."

"Not for very long, I imagine."

She nodded. "Indeed." Pause. "You have been very generous with your time today. You are doubtlessly eager to put this day behind you."

He canted his head. "Why do you say that?"

"I'm certain you did not appreciate the earlier spectacle with . . ." She gestured vaguely.

"That bastard?"

She jerked at the use of profanity. Not because she was particularly offended, but because she had not expected that from him. It seemed so out of his very dignified character. So very unrestrained and he was the epitome of restraint. She grimaced. The very antithesis of Nora.

He shook his head. "Don't give him another thought." His lips twisted wryly. "Believe me, I won't."

"He knew the duke. *Knows* the duke . . ."

"If the man was an important person to Birchwood I would have already met him."

She nodded, trying to let his words soothe her, but she was still stuck on the notion of how her presence was only bringing discomfort to his orderly and noble life. Certainly she had not thought of him when she barged her way into his world, but now she thought of him.

Now she thought of him a great deal.

Studying him, she admitted that she liked his face. She liked all of him. His face. His form. His large and capable hands.

When she stared at him, she felt a deep pulsing tug in her abdomen. It was most unusual—nothing she had experienced before.

She had not thought him to be the manner of man to appeal to her tastes, but there it was. Attraction. A troubling hypothesis. Not that she felt attraction for someone. She had no problem with that in theory. She was a scientist by nature. As a scientist she was open to different experiences. Just because she was not disposed to marriage did not mean she was uninterested in the possibility of a tryst with a pleasing partner.

Yes, radical thinking for a properly bred lady. She knew that, but she had long ago accepted herself as unconventional. She should shy from the notion of amorous congress outside the bounds of matrimony, but she did not.

The very act seemed a natural thing. What was more fundamental than copulation? Her sisters appeared to enjoy it, if the secret smiles and lingering looks and secret touches they shared with their husbands signified anything. Yes, they did not think she noticed that which seemed inherent to the nature of desire—total blindness to the world around you.

Nora was not averse to the act of fornication in principle, but she was averse to the notion of it with *him*. Attractive or not, he was not a possible candidate. Even if he was receptive for a tryst, which she doubted he was, he was a totally unfit candidate.

The man was rigid and humorless (well, mostly) and skeptical of her medical abilities. Not to mention wholly ineligible.

He was courting another female—a veritable paragon of womanhood. He was practically betrothed to her, and Nora would certainly never dally with a man already engaged with another woman. She possessed too much dignity for that.

It only underscored what she already knew. It was time to go.

She glanced to the window. The carriage started to roll slowly forward. They were moving again.

"Miss Langley . . . Nora." At the sound of her Christian name on his lips, she started a bit and looked back at him.

He had never addressed her so intimately. That was not like the reserved Mr. Sinclair she knew him to be at all.

His dark eyes glowed in the dim interior of their carriage and in that moment he appeared almost . . . feral. A beast prowling the dark wood. The sudden notion struck her. Perhaps he wasn't all she thought. "The way you stood up to that bastard?" he murmured in a low, growly voice. "Where did that girl go? I did not think she cared what some man thought."

It took her a moment to recall they had been discussing the outraged gentleman and the ugly scene back at the hospital.

"I don't care what *he* thinks," she responded, and then, before she could consider it, she blurted out with: "I care what *you* think."

Her declaration hung between them, the words suspended in the heavy, charged air.

He held her gaze and she looked away once to the window, briefly, and then back at him.

He was still staring at her in that way she felt low and deep in her belly.

It bewildered her. She had never *felt* another person's gaze before. How was that even possible?

She moistened her lips. "I don't want to cause any difficulties for you."

His liquid-dark eyes seeped deeper into her. "Since when do you care about being a pain in my arse?"

She gasped and then let out a single hiccup of laughter. "I care."

Something that looked suspiciously like a smile shaped his mouth. "Hm."

"I know how important it is for you to establish yourself as the duke's heir and bring honor to his family."

"That is true, but it has naught to do with you."

She flinched even though there was no unkindness in his words, just cold truth.

It has naught to do with you.

He might as well have said *you* have *naught to do with me*. It was tantamount to that bit of dismissal.

Some of her reaction must have shown on her face, for his voice softened as he said, "My rise or fall as the future Duke of Birchwood will be on my head. Don't hold yourself responsible for such an occurrence."

"That may be, but I'm certain you do not relish episodes like today." With people gawking and whispering and no doubt in a hurry to be off to gossip about him.

"Any talk of that bit of drama will subside," he reassured with a shrug. "Something bigger will come along. Always does."

The carriage suddenly jerked forward hard and came to an abrupt halt.

"Oof!" The motion launched her from her seat and tossed her across the space directly into Sinclair's lap.

It was an uncomfortable position. Her legs were awkwardly arranged, her knees on the floor between them, her face buried in his chest, nose bumping smartly against him.

"Miss Langley!" he exclaimed, his hands seizing her arms and pulling her up as though she were featherlight, which she knew was not the case. "Are you hurt?"

"N-no." She gave a tremulous laugh. "This London traffic is a hazardous thing."

He hauled her up higher against him, plopping her down on his lap. Thankfully, it eased the discomfort of her cramped legs as he settled her over him, however much inappropriate.

There was no need for him to hold her like this. Not any longer. There was no need for them to be tangled up like this, however cozy and exciting. And yet she couldn't move . . . and he wasn't lifting herself or himself away.

"I'm fine," she reassured him, releasing an agitated breath and rubbing at the tip of her nose.

Concern was writ all over his face, creasing his brow. Those deep-set eyes of his, so dark and intent, churned her insides. His hands flexed on her arms, and she looked down, noting how very much she was splayed against him, indecently nestled in his lap, her skirts a great pile of muslin around them.

She inhaled, sucking in a great breath, and *that* was a mistake. He smelled so very nice. Like soap and leather and . . . *him*. Even with her hand over her nose, his scent enveloped her.

His gaze flicked to her hand, and he frowned. "Did you hurt your nose?"

"Bumped it," she murmured.

His hands flexed anew, tightening ever so slightly on her biceps. The warmth of his palms and fingers penetrated through the fabric of her sleeves. In fact, all of her felt warm, flushed.

She lowered her hand from her face then, not wishing to appear wounded and elicit more of his concern. Her fingers hovered, shaky for a moment between them. She was unsure where to go, where to land. As though compelled by a force outside of herself, she settled her palm flat on him, fingers splayed on the center of his firm chest. His heart beat strong and a bit fast. A lump grew in her throat.

Touching him like this, alone together in the shadowy interior of the carriage, she felt small and feminine and soft in a way she had never felt before. Her softness to his unyielding solidness . . . she simply wanted to sink into him, to take all of him in, to let herself be swallowed up and consumed by him.

Such thoughts were wholly foreign to her. She had never felt this, never imagined she could. She supposed this was what happened to women and men alike when they cast aside their reservations. Desire, the overriding pull to fornicate, was a powerful thing indeed. The scientist in her was intrigued to follow this through and see for herself what all the hullabaloo was about. For research purposes, of course.

And yet she could not deny that the woman in her was equally intrigued. All her most basic parts were sending forth loud signals. The very core of her pulsed with a deep throb that begged for relief, for pressure.

Only this man was not one for dalliance. At least not with her. She let out a sigh. Unfortunate that. On multiple levels, he was not an acceptable candidate on that score. For starters, he far outranked her. Then there was the fact that he was . . . attached to a lady already. A very likeable and lovely young lady. And he did not like Nora. Perhaps she should have begun with that. He might have granted her pardon to stay with him and the Birchwoods, and he might have treated her to a special day, but it did not alter that he found her to be a duplicitous female. That was forever between them.

He lifted a hand and touched her then, his fingers gently stroking her nose. "Doesn't appear bruised."

She shivered a little. Breathing became too difficult. She could not help herself then. She had to move, had to do something to answer the deep throbbing. She shifted, wiggled against him.

A hissed breath escaped him and she felt her eyes widen in her face. Her fingers stirred, the tips exerting the slightest pressure on him. Their gazes locked, held interminably, and she felt like she was drowning. How could any one person have such dark, lush lashes?

His hands moved then, landing on her hips, fisting in her skirts. "So much bloody fabric," he muttered.

A ragged breath escaped her, expelling from her lungs, easing the tightness in her chest but doing nothing to cure the throbbing.

He uncurled his fist from her skirts, loosening his grip, letting go. His warm palm covered the back of her hand entirely, engulfing it where she held it against him. The intimacy of his longer fingers threaded with hers made something other than her core ache. Her heart gave a tiny little squeeze, and that was alarming. She'd thought this was only physical. Simple biology. Nothing that consisted of sentiment. Nothing as complicated as that.

The carriage resumed, rolling forward and jarring her.

They both blinked, severing the spell, for it did feel like a spell. Some enchantment that had thoroughly addled her and made her forget herself—just as he clearly had forgotten himself. There had been nothing of him in this. No glimpse of the taciturn colonel-turned-duke-to-be. No, he'd been as primitive as the beast in the woods.

But that was gone. The carriage was moving again, and Sinclair was back in all his austerity. His hands briefly gripped her waist and set her on the seat opposite from him, his touch perfunctory and brief.

The carriage rolled to a smooth stop. For a moment Nora thought they were delayed again due to congestion, but then she realized they had arrived at Birchwood House.

"We're here," he said unnecessarily, his voice almost overly loud in the closed confines.

Sinclair extended an arm to open the carriage door, reaching it before the groom could. He exited and hopped down deftly, stretching out both hands to assist her. She descended, feeling giddy and breathless from the day's outing. Once beside him, he offered his arm and she accepted, nestling her gloved fingers in the crook of his elbow.

The air between them still felt thick and charged as they made their way up the steps and inside the house. A pair of footmen stepped forward to collect their gloves and hats.

She tried not to look at Sinclair as she slipped her gloves from her fingers and handed them off to the stoic-faced footman.

She tried, not so valiantly, to *not* think of those moments earlier in their carriage. When they had been alone and his face had been so close that she could admire the sooty length of his lashes. When he had hauled her onto his lap and seemed like he wanted to kiss her and get his hands under her skirts. *Heavens.* He'd behaved like he wanted to tear those skirts off her. She dragged in a heavy breath, suddenly feeling overly warm. Goodness. She needed to find Bea and start packing.

She had just untied the ribbons of her bonnet and removed it from her head when the housekeeper appeared, breathless and holding her side as though she suffered a stitch. "Mr. Sinclair. Miss Langley. Thank goodness you're both home."

"What is it, Mrs. Blankenship?" Sinclair asked.

"It's the duchess. She's ill and taken to her bed."

Sinclair turned his gaze on Nora. He did not need to say anything. Words were not necessary. His expression said it all.

It was time for her to do what she had come here to do.

Chapter 16

*C*onstantine took Nora by the hand and hastened to the duchess's bedchamber, his pulse pounding anxiously in his ears.

The duke was sitting at his wife's bedside when they entered the room. His eyes landed on Constantine instantly. "Where have you been?" he demanded. When his gaze alighted on Nora some of the panic ebbed from his bloodshot eyes. "Ah, you're here, gel. Thank heavens. Help her. Please."

Constantine took Nora's arm and led her closer to the bed.

The duke vacated the chair so that she could use it to sit closer and examine the duchess who reclined listlessly in her regal bed.

The duke took up position beside him along the wall where he stood a safe distance from the colossal bed at the center of the chamber. "Where were you?" he grumbled, his resentment sharp on the air.

"I took Nora . . . er, Miss Langley to visit Middlesex."

Birchwood looked at him askance. "The hospital? Why? Is the girl ill?"

"No. I thought she might like to observe the surgical theater there. It is quite renowned."

The duke's eyes narrowed and he looked at Constantine long and hard before facing forward again. "We needed you here." He nodded at Nora. "We needed *her*. Is that not why she is here? To help my Maude? Not to go off gallivanting with you?" The duke's lips tightened, almost disappearing before they released and he spoke again. "What is this girl to you?"

Constantine could only stare. He had no response. The question was absurd.

After some moments, he finally found his voice. "Nor—Miss Langley? She is no one to me. She's here because she is a very skilled herbalist." The words felt wrong somehow. He studied Nora as she bent over the duchess, her hands gently probing and touching the duchess's inert body.

She was not *no one*.

She was someone. Someone who drove him to distraction and made his skin feel too hot and too tight over his bones.

"You best leave her be then. She is here for my Maude. Not for you and whatever oats you seek to sow. Lady Elise is for you. Busy yourself with wooing her."

He nodded. "Of course."

It was far easier to agree with the man. Especially as he stood fretting, clearly distraught over his wife. A wife who looked alarmingly pale and listless beneath Nora's ministrations.

The duchess moaned softly, clearly beset with pain. She turned her face into the pillow as though hoping to muffle the sound.

Birchwood tensed beside him. "I can't lose her. I won't survive that. Now that our sons are gone, she's all I have." He faced Constantine while nodding toward the bed, toward Nora. "You brought her here."

Constantine sighed and nodded. "I did." A fact he was coming to regret.

"She has to heal her. She must."

"I know she will try."

The old man seized his hand in a surprisingly strong, *crushing* grip. "Not good enough, lad. You see it done." His eyes were red with emotion. "See. It. Done."

NORA LEFT THE duchess's bedside only once and that was to collect her bag and all the ingredients she needed to prepare remedies for the afflicted lady. She had the maids erect a work table for her in the duchess's chamber. Nora was prepared to try anything that might work. She had several options in mind.

None, however, seemed to work.

That was her conclusion the following day when the duchess still moaned and writhed in agony in her bed, no relief achieved.

Oh, Nora's lavender rosemary ointment and salt lemon tincture gave some ease, but only for a short time. She knew her remedies treated the symptoms. She still did not know what afflicted the duchess, only that her aches seemed to go bone deep. The older woman was able to indicate that her shoulders and arms bore the brunt of her pain. Without properly understanding what plagued her, Nora feared she could never cure her.

She was poring over one of Papa's books she had brought from home when the door to the chamber opened. The duke marched in the room without casting her a glance, leading a tall, impeccably attired gentleman. They walked a direct line to the bed.

The stranger settled the bag he carried upon

the edge of the bed beside the duchess. He pressed a hand to her brow and clucked his tongue sympathetically. "How are you feeling, Your Grace? Not quite yourself, I hear?"

The duchess opened her eyes. She seemed to stare at the man with a decided lack of focus. Eventually, she let out a huff of discomfort and rolled over onto her side.

Opening his bag, the man started digging inside it. It took all her will not to step forward and demand his identity and purpose. He lifted a vial and poured some of the liquid into a spoon.

At that point, she could not stop herself. She took several steps forward. "What is that?"

The man looked over his shoulder and regarded her with an arrogant expression. "'Tis laudanum. It will relax her."

She frowned. Apparently the man was a doctor. A doctor the Duke of Birchwood did not see fit to introduce to her. She shifted on her feet, suddenly uncomfortable in her own skin.

She cringed as she watched him pour a very generous dose of laudanum for the duchess.

Unlike many physicians, Papa had not been a devotee of the medicine. He found that patients became too dependent on opiates and he had believed them to be altering to mind and body.

He'd used them only in the most extreme of circumstance and she had never seen him administer such a substantial dose to anyone.

She bit her lip, frowning down at the duchess. Whatever the duchess's condition, it appeared to be chronic. She could very easily become dependent on the drug for relief for her recurring pain. In that event, she would not even be herself anymore. She would just be a shell of a person craving her next dose.

She stretched out a hand. "Wait. I do not think—"

"That will be all, Miss Langley," the duke's voice whipped across the air. "Your *services* are no longer needed here." She flinched. He had never spoken to her in such a way. The man fairly sneered the word *services*. And his eyes . . .

He looked at her as though she were something to be scraped from the bottom of his boot. It was cutting . . . and an effective reminder of where she ranked here, in this place, among these people—of just how little value she held.

Just beyond the duke, the doctor slipped a hand beneath the duchess's neck and lifted her head so that she could drink the medicine.

Her shoulders slumped. It was done then.

"Now," the doctor proclaimed and he resumed

rummaging through his bag. "Let's fetch a bowl so that we may bleed her." He cast a quick glance around, his gaze alighting on a maid lurking nearby. He nodded to her. "A bowl and some additional linens, please."

"No! No bloodletting." She lunged to grasp his arm. "She is too weak for that."

The doctor looked down at her hand with wide eyes and a faintly curling upper lip. "Your Grace? Who is this . . . *person* and why is she touching me?"

Person was a kind substitution for what he really thought. She knew that at once from the way he looked her up and down.

"No one. She is no one." The duke sent a pointed look to her hand. "Release Sir Anthony at once, Miss Langley, and leave this room."

She is no one. His words reverberated like a tolling clang in her head. Here, in this place, she was no one. All she would ever be to these people was no one.

She slid her hand from the man's arm, feeling a bit stunned at the duke's rudeness.

"Your Grace," a deep voice intoned. "Have a care."

Nora twisted around to find the source. Her gaze landed on Sinclair. She had not noticed his arrival in the chamber, but, of course, he was here. He was the duke's shadow, acclimated to his new role, never far away. Except his usual stoic demeanor was gone. He looked quietly furious.

"I beg your pardon?" Birchwood sputtered.

"Miss Langley is *my* guest. Have a care how you address her."

Nora looked back and forth between the two men, sensing an exchange passing between them, a dialogue she could not understand.

"*Your* guest?"

"Yes." The single word fell dark and heavy, and something physically came over the duke's body. The older man settled back on his heels, his shoulders easing, sinking as he stared wide-eyed at Sinclair.

"Come now," Sinclair said gently beside her, turning away from Birchwood. "Let's take some air. You've been cooped up in this room long enough. You must be overly tired."

She looked helplessly at the wan duchess in the middle of the bed, reluctant to leave her. Her face was drawn tight in pain. Her head rolled side to side on the pillow, her lips muttering non-sensical words. At least she was unaware of what was going on around her. She was spared their squabbling.

He settled his hand on her elbow and tugged her away until she let go of the doctor. She nodded numbly and let herself be led from the room.

Of course, it was time to leave the chamber. Just as it was time to leave this place—this house, this city.

She had not succeeded. She had not accomplished the one thing she was supposed to do here.

"You did your best."

She slipped her arm free of Sinclair and looked up at him. "You don't believe that. You did not think I could help her in the first place."

He shook his head. "I don't know that anyone can help her." He nodded back toward the chamber. "He has attended her several times and he hasn't cured her yet. Perhaps no one can."

And yet Nora had been so confidant. Arrogant even. Her disappointment was keen. She crossed her arms across her chest. "Since I am no longer needed here, I'll leave on the morrow."

He blinked. "What?"

"It is clear my purpose here is at an end." She swallowed, regretting the tightness in her voice. She did not want him to think she was hurt. She did not want his pity.

For a moment he appeared astonished, quietly

staring at her. Then, he said, "You needn't rush away. The duchess quite enjoys your company."

"I am not a hired companion, Mr. Sinclair."

Of course, that was how they viewed her, how she best fit in here. As a glorified servant. One step above the downstairs staff, but not one of them. Never one of them.

She did not know why that bothered her so much. She had not given much thought to rank before. Perhaps it was the fact that she was so obviously not in the same class as Mr. Sinclair. That he was far removed from her. That they were not equal in the eyes of Society.

"I am certain I am missed at home." Perhaps. *But likely not.* Her sisters were both caught up in their own happy lives. "I can be of use there."

He looked at her almost in wonder. "That's important to you."

"What is?"

"Being useful."

She shrugged and then nodded. "Is that so extraordinary?"

He released a rough little laugh. "Yes. It is. You are an extraordinary female, Miss Langley."

She exhaled, trying not to reveal how very flattered she felt. She ought not to feel that way. On the surface, extraordinary seemed an impressive jump from being characterized as a *no one*, but she suspected it still was not what proper young girls aspired to be.

Extraordinary could be translated as odd, eccentric. All things she had been called, and each time they had not been intended as compliments.

"I apologize for not helping the duchess. I was arrogant in thinking I—"

"No." He shook his head. "You did all you could—"

"No. I promised you I could help her. I failed." She would not allow him to brush aside her duty—the duty she herself had chosen. She had insisted on it, in fact. "If you want to renege on our arrangement, I understand."

"Arrangement?" He looked befuddled.

"I proved myself ineffectual." She clenched her jaw. It was difficult to admit that. Especially when she still considered herself better and more skilled than the doctor administering to the duchess right now, using his antiquated methods to treat her. "It is only right that you reveal my deception to all and sundry."

He exhaled and dragged a hand through his dark hair. "I was wrong to threaten you with that."

"No. You were doing what you thought right. Protecting people."

Protecting people from me.

Before he could open his mouth and say something kind that was probably untrue and motivated only by pity, she added, "I think you're quite right. I am very tired. I think I shall go rest a spell. Good day to you, Mr. Sinclair."

That said, she spun and departed, mindful not to look back.

Chapter 17

*A*s Nora suspected, Bea was quite disappointed to learn they would be departing for home.

"We have not been here nearly long enough," she protested, getting in Nora's way and being generally unhelpful as Nora went ahead and started packing since Bea seemed disinclined.

A pair of servants had returned all her things from the duchess's chamber. A clear sign that felt like a slap. She was clearly expected to leave the lady alone.

"I have been here *too* long, I think."

"What of the duchess?" Bea's eyes snapped with accusation. "I thought you were going to help her?"

Nora felt her failure keenly. She'd been overly confidant. "I tried. I tried and failed."

"Nonsense. You only tried for a day. You cannot have exhausted every option."

Shaking her head, Nora moved to her dressing table and peered inside her bag. The servants had returned it to her, after they had ostensibly tossed everything inside it with little regard. *And why should they treat her with politeness or hold her in regard when their master of the house so obviously did not?*

She caught a whiff of various herbs and knew something had either broken or spilled inside the bag.

Sighing, she set to work organizing it as it had been before, ignoring Bea who continued to argue the merits of staying at Birchwood House.

Nora grabbed a linen cloth and attempted to wipe up the ointment that had spilled in the bottom. Tears burned her eyes for some unaccountable reason. She blinked them back and told herself to stop such nonsense. There was no reason to be emotional.

Her hand brushed a vial that was on its side, tucked in the corner of the bag where it had rolled. She pulled it out to identify it and stilled, staring down at it in her hand.

She sucked in a little breath. She'd forgotten

it was in there. She did not remember packing it. She would not have done so. She must have grabbed it when she was taking items from her cabinet, where she stored it with so many of her tonics and salves.

Marian thought she had destroyed it. Nora had done nothing to correct that misapprehension.

Marian had advised her to do so, insisted, in fact . . . even knowing Nora could simply replicate it and make a fresh batch. She claimed she would feel safer in the house if the tonic did not exist, if it was not sitting somewhere on one of Nora's shelves. As though it was a keg of gunpowder that could erupt and explode accidentally.

Nora had not, however, destroyed it. Of course not.

She'd kept the original mixture, feeling almost loyal to it. It was the reason Charlotte and Kingston came together. At least initially.

She studied the little bronze bottle, turning it over in her hand, well aware of the power that was inside it.

She had promised Marian she would never use it again.

"Miss Nora? Are you listening to me?"

"Hm?" Apparently Bea had been talking to her.

Nora shook her head. No, she had not heard a word the girl had said. She could only stare at the small vial and consider it for what it was. Charlotte had been her unwitting test subject.

Bea approached and peered at what she held in her hand. "What is that?"

"Something I concocted over a year ago for Charlotte . . . to ease the pains of her menses."

Bea perked up. "Indeed. Does it work?"

"It eased her monthly pains, yes," she admitted, stifling a wince. Indeed, it had eliminated Char's monthly aches, but it replaced them with aches of another fashion.

"Might it help the duchess?" Bea looked at her hopefully, her eyes wide with inquiry.

She angled her head contemplatively. "It's much too . . . untested. Charlotte is the only one who tried it." Nora would want to know more about the duchess's condition before she dosed her with the elixir. It would be too risky otherwise.

Bea reached for it. "You want me to try—"

"No!" Nora snapped her hand shut into a fist and tucked her arm behind her. "No, thank you." The last thing she needed was Bea lost to the throes of desire and accosting some poor unaware footman.

"You needn't shout," Bea grumbled, moving away. "I'm only saying, if you have something that mitigates pain, then why are you keeping it from the duchess? Hasn't she been through enough? Poor woman. She is in great pain."

Nora uncurled her fingers and brought her hand back around to look down and examine the tiny bronze vial resting so innocently in her palm. *Why not indeed?*

The brew did, in fact, numb pain with no adverse consequences. She thought about that for a moment and mentally amended. No *long-standing* adverse consequences. It just happened to have one pesky side effect. A pesky *potential* side effect, she again amended. That was an important distinction. Who knew how the elixir would interact with another person? Everyone differed in their individual body composition.

What were the odds that Nora's tonic would overcome the duchess's good sense and modesty and turn her into . . .

Nora couldn't even finish the thought. It was so ludicrous. The proper and dignified sixty-year-old lady would not lose her decorum and become mad with lust. It was impossible to envision such a thing.

Charlotte had been modest and prudent. Nora ignored the reminder, her mind continuing down a path of rationalization.

Could it really affect the duchess in such an extreme manner?

Perhaps if Nora reduced the dosage and started with a small fraction of what she administered to Charlotte?

Perhaps . . .

No. She gave a single swift shake of her head. Marian would tell her it was reckless and irresponsible. She could almost hear her sister's voice in her ears.

Nora resumed exploring all her various remedies. Remedies that never turned anyone into a lust-afflicted beast.

She vowed not to think on it again. It was much too risky for the duchess.

Besides. She was done here. Soon she'd be back in Brambledon. Back to her life, her routines. It was doubtful she'd ever step foot in this city again. Warrington certainly was not compelled to visit Town.

She'd be gone and it would be the last she ever saw of Sinclair. She ignored the small pang in her chest that prompted. Perhaps he'd reveal her deception. Perhaps not.

Whatever the situation, she would finish packing and be on her way.

DESPITE ALL INTENTIONS, Nora could not stop thinking about that tiny bronze vial. All her things were packed, ready for departure on the morrow, but sleep was elusive.

She finally gave up. Flinging back the counterpane, she hopped from bed and snatched her night rail where it rested at the foot of the bed. Wrapping herself in it and tightening the belt at her waist, she crept out into the corridor.

Nora stopped before Sinclair's door and shifted uneasily on her feet. She lifted her hand to knock and then hesitated, pulling back. She bit her lip in contemplation.

She knew it was unseemly to visit him in his bedchamber, but considering it had to do with the well-being of the duchess, she thought decorum could be set aside for a much-needed discussion with Sinclair.

She came here for one reason, after all. She might very well have a way to help the duchess. The lady was in acute pain. Even with possible side effects, it was only fair that she present the treatment option to Sinclair. A conversation was justified. More than justified. It was necessary.

Her original purpose in coming here had been forgotten or at least pushed aside since her arrival. Not through any manner of neglect. The duchess had simply been in good health, seemingly so, and Nora had allowed herself to become complacent. She'd allowed her head to be turned by an afternoon jaunt with a handsome man.

Her holiday was over.

Now it was time to work. She wasn't running for home with her tail tucked in her skirts until she had exhausted all options on the duchess's behalf.

Forget about propriety and the rules that applied to the proper ladies of Society. Nora had no such aspirations. She never had.

In another life, perhaps if Nora had been a son, she would have gone on to be a doctor like Papa. There would have been no barriers to stop her, no dour-faced men at the helm of medical institutions to say she was not allowed.

Ironically, Phillip, her brother who was soon to finish at Eton, was not in the least interested in such a pursuit. It was maddening. He would have been allowed to train to be a doctor whilst she could not.

"Enough of this," she murmured under her breath and brought her knuckles against the door, rapping on the wood.

The dinner hour was over. Not that anyone had eaten downstairs in the lavish dining room. Not tonight. As the duchess was ill, the servants had delivered trays to everyone at their various locations.

Bea had eaten in her room with her. They paused amid packing. The servants had delivered their trays with clear disapproval writ all over their faces.

She was careful not to knock too loudly. The dinner hour was over, but she knew the staff was still up and about.

No sense alerting the household of her presence at Sinclair's door. They might leap to the conclusion that she was looking for an assignation with the duke's heir. She could well imagine *that* gossip. They would think she was set on becoming his mistress. Of course that would be their salacious conclusion. In no way could they imagine the likes of her in Sinclair's life in a conventionally romantic way. He was one breath from the altar with the very admired Lady Elise.

Con opened the door to her knock. "Nora?" He blinked those inky lashes over his dark eyes. "What are you doing here?"

"I've been contemplating the duchess's condition, and . . ." Her voice faded away at what she was about to impart. She could still hear Marian's voice in her head . . . both her sisters' voices actually, pleading with her not to do it. Not to say it.

"And?" he prompted.

She took a deep, fortifying breath. "And I think I have something that could help her."

Chapter 18

*W*hy did you not mention this tonic of yours sooner?" Constantine asked, peering down at her with suspicion.

Upon finding her outside his door, he had pulled her inside his chamber lest someone stumble upon them and draw the wrong conclusions.

Now they were alone. Together, in his room.

He swallowed thickly and very deliberately looked away from her face.

"It's still very . . . *experimental*," she replied.

Something in her voice made him glance again at her face. Was it his imagination or was she blushing? That was decidedly new. He would never have considered her the blushing type. In fact, he had never seen her look as nervous or agitated as she was now.

At the hospital, she'd watched from the gallery without blinking or looking away or turning the slightest shade of green as a very nearly naked body was cut open.

But now she appeared discomfited. Something about this tonic discomfited her.

"Experimental in what way?"

She pulled her bottom lip between her teeth and then let it pop back out. "My sister tried it. Charlotte. It had the most . . . unusual effect on her."

"Your sister Charlotte? That is not Warrington's wife?"

"No, it is not. Charlotte married Warrington's stepbrother. She lives nearby. In Brambledon."

"Is she ill?"

"Oh, no. She is hale and hearty." Nora nodded assuredly. "She was just suffering from some aches and took this tonic the one time." She opened her palm to reveal a little bronze vial in her hand.

He peered down at it thoughtfully. "And did it relieve her pain?"

"Um, in a manner."

"Cease speaking in riddles, Nora. Can this help or not?" he snapped, determined to get to the heart of the matter so that she could soon leave his room.

Her presence here was much too disconcerting . . . in the same way he had felt with her in the carriage. It was as though close quarters with her addled his thoughts and had him doing things like studying her lips and her very fine eyes and the tempting shape of her. It was very wrong of him. It should be Lady Elise's lips that fascinated him.

She bristled at his brusque tone, and he knew he'd hit a nerve with it. "The potion has side effects. Or rather, one particular side effect."

He frowned. "But you said your sister is well. These side effects mustn't be too terrible."

"Um. I suppose that depends."

He fought down his exasperation. It was not like her to prevaricate. If anything she was too bold and direct. "Please elaborate."

"You won't believe me." Her chin went up a fraction. "No one does at first. My sister Marian did not."

Presumably, she did now. "Try me."

She assessed him as though evaluating him for his sincerity. At last, she spoke. "The tonic afflicts one . . ."

"Yes?" he prompted.

"It acts as a trigger for one's desires."

He digested that.

Making certain he understood her correctly, he asked, "You're saying that this tonic of yours fills one with lust?"

She nodded. "It overtakes them, yes. The most acute lust. Terrible and—"

"Well, right there you are confused because lust is not terrible. That is not the nature of it at all."

Her lips parted as she looked up at him, and the air crackled, popping over the surface of his skin as he stared at that mouth of hers, such a deep rose color that it looked perpetually swollen. As though those lips had been thoroughly ravished . . . and begged to be ravished again.

Only a few inches separated them. A few inches of space between him and that pillowy mouth.

Bloody hell.

He should not be discussing *lust*, of all topics, with *this* female.

Especially alone. At night. In his bedchamber. Doing so provoked all manner of feelings and thoughts uncustomary to him.

He'd lived a sensible life, and he had thought to continue on that path even as the future Duke of Birchwood. Becoming a duke presented new duties and responsibilities, certainly, but it did not change him. Not intrinsically. Constantine was the same man he'd been *before* receiving word to return home and take up the mantle as heir to the Birchwood legacy.

Even whilst in the army, he was circumspect, never engaging in the services of the many camp followers. That was not to say he lived as a monk. He simply had never been a man ruled by his cock.

But in this moment, he felt entirely subject to his baser instincts.

Nora Langley brought out his feral side. His body hummed and pulsed with the urge to crush that mouth under his.

She roused his caveman instincts and he did not care for it. Not one little bit.

Her tongue darted out to moisten her lips and he felt that small act twisting his gut.

"It is if it goes unquenched. It can be terrible." Her throat worked as she swallowed. "At least that's what I was told."

"By your sister?"

She nodded.

He cleared his thick throat. "So you have no personal experience with lust then?"

Bloody. Hell. The question escaped him before he could stop himself.

He did not flirt. And he most especially did

not flirt with young women with whom he was stuck in a comprising position.

The moment the words were out he wished he could snatch them back and stuff the words down his throat.

Her eyes widened, clearly startled.

He did not want to know of her experience or lack thereof. Very well. That was not entirely accurate. Truthfully, either knowledge was exciting. To know that she had experience thrilled him. To know she was an innocent thrilled him, too.

Bloody hell.

She thrilled him. The. End.

"I can only speak of my sister's experience with the tonic. She's the only subject to have tested it. I've been uneasy subjecting it to anyone else." She might have attempted it on herself, but she, fortunately, had been in good health with no pains or aches, and, admittedly . . . her sisters had put a bit of fear in her.

What happened if she was afflicted with raging lusts? She had no one to slake her desires upon.

What if she tested it and then assaulted a stranger? Someone she was not even remotely attracted to? It seemed a grave risk.

Ideally, if the tonic were to be tested again one of her sisters should take it for they had husbands only too happy to satisfy any raging desires that should overcome them. But neither one would agree to that even if they were here.

In fact, ever since Nora had dosed Char with the tonic, her sisters had been rather distrustful about taking any of her herbal remedies. It was rather galling. They'd always trusted her before.

"You said the tonic eased your sister's pain?"

"Yes. Yes, it did," she confirmed.

Charlotte had not felt the misery of her cramping belly. That much was true. She had felt nothing save the deepest arousal. At least that was what she had claimed. Whether the pain had been truly absent or replaced with arousal, who was to say? And did it matter if the pain was no longer felt?

"Then it seems clear what we must do."

She blinked and angled her head sharply. "Is it?"

"Indeed. I will take your tonic."

Chapter 19

*N*ora stared at him for several moments, her mouth working as her brain searched for the proper reply to his outrageous announcement. "You are mad."

"Why would you say that?" he asked in all mildness, as though he had not just declared a lunatic idea.

"Y—you . . . cannot take it."

Absolutely not. He could *not* take the tonic. Just the notion of him . . . the very austere Mr. Sinclair all hot eyed and titillated was unthinkable. She swallowed thickly.

Unthinkable . . . and yet exciting when she did permit herself to think of it. She envisioned him as he had been in the carriage, all deep dark eyes and gravelly voice that she felt like a caress.

Except in her imaginings she would visualize him touching her.

His hand would land on her ankle and slide up, up, up . . . slipping beneath her skirts, skimming over her stockings until he reached her garters. And there he would make haste, ripping the ribbons free, shredding them in animal speed so that he could get to her skin, get to her. Her breathing fell faster. *Oh, dear.*

"Miss Langley?"

She snapped free of her little fantasy and looked at him, the very controlled Mr. Sinclair. This very restrained and self-possessed gentleman would not appreciate any remedy that robbed him of his control. Who would, for that matter?

"Yes?"

"You need a test subject, and as the tonic is for a member of my family and I am the one responsible for you being here—"

"Are you the one responsible for my presence here though?" She had rather forced herself on him here. Looking back at her behavior, she felt a small dose of shame. She could still hear the duke's voice in her head, dismissing her so coldly, so imperiously. He'd made her feel small . . . so small and unwelcome that she wanted to flee this place with what dignity she still possessed.

He ignored her interruption and continued, "I should be the one to take it." He flattened a hand to his chest covered only by the elegant lawn of his shirt. No jacket. No vest. This was the most casual she had ever seen him. Casual and loose and she rather liked him this way—disheveled. "I should be the one," he insisted.

She could not allow that to happen under any circumstance. At least not without Lady Elise on hand. She should be the one, of course, to help him if the tonic affected him as it did her sister. Otherwise he would be left to the agony of his unfulfilled desires.

And what if Lady Elise did not help him with that? They might be courting, but that did not mean the elegant lady would cast aside all propriety to satisfy his cravings.

"Let us consider this," she began. "If the tonic affects you—"

"Makes me aroused," he clarified.

She nodded. "Er, yes. Then what?"

"Then I endure it."

He made it sound so easy. Only she knew better. She knew what happened to Char. "What if you cannot? It might not be that simple."

"What are you suggesting then?"

Nora did not imagine that his eyes suddenly looked darker and felt more intense, more focused on her. A subtle energy crackled off him. She swallowed again. "I am suggesting that you not do it."

He nodded once. "I am doing it."

She exhaled. "Then perhaps we should send for Lady Elise."

He started a bit at that, his eyebrows furrowing. "Why would we do that?"

"Well." She fluttered her hand. "So she can be on hand." He stared at her blankly, prompting her to elaborate further. "In case you are overcome and find yourself in need . . ." Her voice faded and mortifying heat swept up her face.

Now he was staring at her as though *she* were the mad one.

"I cannot compromise Lady Elise, even were she willing, which is doubtful."

The heat increased in her face. She felt foolish now.

Of course Lady Elise would not dally outside the bounds of matrimony. She was a lady through and through. Not to mention that dragon of an aunt probably never even let her out of her sight.

He continued, "If it does affect me as you fear, I shall simply endure it until it fades."

Simply endure it? She eyed him skeptically,

recalling her sister writhing on the bed, desperate for satisfaction, for release.

"Don't look so skeptical, Miss Langley."

She nodded, looking down again at the small bronze vial in her palm. A breath shuddered through her. She felt as though she toed the brink of a great precipice. She was about to go right over the edge and she didn't know what waited at the bottom of the other side. "You are determined to do this."

"I am."

She sucked in a deep breath. "Very well. Let's fetch a spoon."

TWO HOURS LATER, Nora knocked briskly, as loud as she dared, on his bedchamber door. She had not seen or heard a peep from him since he took the tonic. She had to reassure herself he was well.

Sending a quick glance left and right down the empty corridor, she bit her lip in consternation. Here she stood yet again, braving scandal to have a word with Sinclair.

She grew only more concerned as the minutes ticked past and she stood hovering before his door, shifting impatiently on her feet.

She knocked again, slightly louder, slightly more insistent. "Mr. Sinclair?"

It was strange addressing him so formally as she had just administered an aphrodisiac to him. That seemed the kind of thing that people on a first name basis would do.

"Are you . . . well?" she asked in hushed tones, unsure what to ask of him precisely. *Are you overcome from arousal and wishing for death to end the torment?*

Something clattered inside the room followed by a muffled groan.

"Mr. Sinclair," she said again, more desperately this time. Not caring for propriety, she seized the latch and tried to open it. No luck. The door was locked. She rattled the latch and called out, "Mr. Sinclair. Open this door."

His muffled voice carried through the barrier of wood. "Go 'way!"

She pulled back, blinking, glaring at the door as though it were alive. *Go away?* That was an impossibility. She could not abandon him to this.

She dropped her hand away from the latch. After a moment's hesitation, she pressed her face close to the door, hoping her voice would better penetrate through the wood that way. "Mr. Sinclair, are you unwell? Let me in at once, sir. You're frightening me."

What if she had poisoned him? *Dear Heavens.* What if he was dead?

His voice called out again, this time much firmer, clearly conveying his agitation. "Go away. Now!"

"Oh," she breathed in keen disapproval.

He was clearly in distress and would not open the door to her even though he obviously required assistance. Stubborn man!

She gave the door a swift kick in a display of pique. Unfortunately that did nothing save bruise her toes.

Standing back with a huff, she propped her hands on her hips and glared at the barrier. She supposed she could find the housekeeper or butler for a master key to gain entry to his chamber. They would oblige if she explained Mr. Sinclair was in some distress and in need of help. It would not be a terribly difficult feat.

But then they would become privy to whatever was happening on the other side of this door, and Sinclair clearly did not want anyone to see him in his present condition otherwise he would not be locked in his chamber. He had told her rather confidently that he would endure whatever was to come. But what if he had underestimated his endurance?

What was his present condition?

It was quiet now on the other side of that door. Too quiet.

Her stomach plummeted as the fear of the unknown beset her. What if he was truly ill? Perhaps he was retching and he thought that was something she could not bear to witness?

She was made of stern stuff, but, of course, he would not realize or understand that. He would not be aware that she had observed retching and all manner of ugly things working beside her father and then later on her own. There could be nothing uglier than lancing one of Mr. Pratt's boils.

Or perhaps it was worse than retching. Perhaps he was dying.

Because of her.

She pressed a hand against her suddenly roiling stomach, willing the queasiness to subside. She resisted the urge to fling herself against the door and beat on it until he opened to her.

Foolish man! She forced the air in and out of her in a controlled manner. *Think, Nora, think.*

She had to find a way inside that room. Except how would she gain entry to his chamber through the door he had barred? She could not simply fly in through his balcony doors like some winged savior.

Through his balcony doors.

Turning, she spun around and raced back to her bedchamber, which happened to be only a couple rooms down from him.

She closed the chamber door firmly behind her and advanced on her balcony. Flinging open the double doors, she stepped out into the spring evening and looked resolutely to her left, examining the course necessary to reach Sinclair's room.

Two other balconies loomed between their rooms, but she could reach his balcony by stepping out onto the small ledge that jutted from the side of the house. She need take only a few steps between each balcony to reach his chamber. She estimated that the length of her foot would mostly fit upon the ledge. Mostly. She hoped.

Before she could change her mind or let fear take hold of her, she found herself straddling the balcony and stepping onto the ledge.

This is madness.

As soon as the thought flitted through her mind, she dismissed it—banished it. She was no feeble lady. She walked miles of countryside every day and had climbed plenty of trees in her lifetime. She could tackle this.

Nora experienced a stab of alarm when she reached the first balcony. That had not been easy. Her skirts hampered her quite a bit and it required some careful maneuvering, but she managed to swing a leg over the railing and drop down, her palms scraping slightly on the chilled stone.

She blew out a breath and shoved to her feet, dusting off her palms. She should have changed, but too late now, and there was no time to waste. She needed to keep going. He needed her. Whether he wanted her help or not, he would have it.

Bulky skirts or not, she continued. She crossed over to the next balcony and then finally reached his, arriving at his balcony door to find it unlocked, thankfully.

She pushed open the door unceremoniously, anxious to see him and verify that he was not in fact on death's doorstep—that she had not poisoned him.

It took her a moment to acclimate to the room. Lamplight filled the chamber, but failed to reach to all the corners as it was a large space, much larger than her own, of course. It boasted a full sitting area with a sofa and a duo of wingback chairs.

The bed was easy to locate. It was a great monstrosity. The covers were rumpled into several messy piles. She stepped closer and then spotted him, spotted a single foot dangling off the bed and the long stretch of a leg leading into his hip. Naked.

All of him was naked.

Not a stitch of clothing covered his person.

His face was turned from her, facing the opposite wall.

She cleared her throat to alert him of her arrival so that he might cover himself.

His head whipped around on the bed and she gasped.

His dark eyes were like obsidian fire. They fixed on her with hot-eyed focus. "Nora," he growled in a voice she had never heard from him before. "Go! Get out!"

Her heart clenched. He was in pain. She had done this to him. She had brought him to this.

"What's amiss?" She stepped forward.

"Stop!" She ignored him and continued forward, forcing her gaze on his face. Not his body. At least she tried . . . and succeeded. Mostly.

"Don't come any closer, damn it!" His face contorted as he lifted his voice.

She halted at the force of that command, frowning. It was not like him to shout.

"Sinclair . . . Constantine," she said slowly, softly speaking his name . . . enjoying far too much the feel of it on her tongue. "You need to let me examine you." She held up her hands as one does to pacify a wild animal, to illustrate that she meant him no harm.

"Did you not hear me? You need to get out of this room, woman. Now!"

She flinched at the bark of his voice, but did not back away. "I'm not leaving you. I'm here to take care of you."

He laughed and the sound was broken and tormented, as jagged and sharp as broken glass. A dreadful sound that tore right through her. There was no way she could leave him in such a state.

The tendons in his throat worked as though struggling to swallow. "You can't help me with this. You were . . . right . . . about that."

She had not wanted to be right. She had hoped she would be wrong because now she was faced with this—with him like *this*. And he was her responsibility. Even if he had insisted on taking the tonic and ignoring her advice.

She lifted her chin with forced bravado. "I am the person most equipped in this house to help you, good sir. You must know that."

He groaned as though someone had stuck a hot poker to his flesh—his lovely manly flesh. Tight and smooth flesh stretched over a body that was muscled and well formed. Especially the curve of those buttocks. They were nicely rounded and tight, flexing in a tantalizing manner with his movements.

Her eyes widened with the realization that she was ogling him. She wrenched her gaze back to his face.

"Be gone, woman! Do you see me? Do you see this?" He rolled fully to face her then, lying on his side so she had a full frontal view of him. "Do you see? You cannot help me."

And she did see.

She saw everything.

Every shocking thing.

Chapter 20

*T*here was no staring at his face. Even as handsome as it was, such a thing was impossible. His very erect manhood jutted out from between his legs. Of course she could look nowhere else.

Saliva flooded her mouth. Her lips parted and she worked her jaw, searching for something to say, but it did no good. Words were insignificant. Her mouth was watering as though she'd just scented a nine-course feast replete with all her favorite foods.

She may be a maid still, but when one worked in the business of healing, one observed a multitude of unclothed bodies—even in this era of moral correctness.

Working alongside Papa, she had seen plenty

of naked bodies and observed more than one man's phallus. And yet no body had ever affected her like this.

No man's member had ever looked like this. To begin with, they had all been flaccid. This was a far cry from that.

His rod was . . . large, dark plum in color, the head swollen and angry-looking, ravenous for its release. His hand shot there, gripping it, seizing it in a punishing grip. The sight should have made her cringe, but she felt only a violent tug low in her belly in response. She had the mad urge to brush his hand aside and replace it with her own—to wrap her fingers around him and learn his texture for herself.

She suddenly felt as though she were afflicted with a fever, all of her overly warm, parts of her strangely achy.

She took several halting steps toward the bed.

His liquid dark eyes went wide. "What are you doing? Get out!" Clearly he had thought the sight of him like this would send her fleeing . . . as it would have done for any other gently bred female.

She knew what this was. She'd witnessed her sister Charlotte at its peak, lost to the agony of desire. She knew it would get only worse. Unless he reached his release.

"Are you in a great deal of . . . discomfort?"

He made a choking sound. "Your sister was not exaggerating its power."

"But I cut the dose in half."

Dear heavens . . . what had her sister endured?

As though he read her mind, he choked out, "I pity how your sister must have felt for this is misery."

Or perhaps it worked differently on a man if half a dose resulted in this? Or perhaps it varied simply per individual?

He arched his neck on the bed with a moan and tightened his grip around his manhood. The swollen head went darker and she felt another tug low in her belly, deeper than before. Deeper and pulsing, begging for the pressure to be assuaged.

The lean lines of his body were stretched taut on display, muscles bunching, sinew pulling. He was a fine specimen. She told herself this was only a clinical observation, that she was not admiring him in a licentious way even if she was feeling the telltale signs of arousal herself. Even if she was suffering from shortness of breath. Even if she was imagining putting her hands on him. That was simply a physiological response. As a scientist she could appreciate that.

Nora took a bracing gulp of breath. This was not about her. She was not under the influence of various elements. She was a healer and he required healing. It was as simple as that.

She swallowed against the sudden lump in her throat.

She could help him. That was what she did, after all. Where she excelled. She owed him that much.

She approached tentatively, stopping at the edge of the bed.

His dark eyes fastened on her as a spasm rolled through his body. He still gripped his member, pulling and tugging on it in a way that made her cringe. "Go away, Nora." Then quieter, "Please."

"I can't do that." She eased down on the bed. "Let me help. I owe you that."

His nostrils flared as though the sudden nearness of her was too much.

"Mr. Sin—" She stopped, catching herself. At this point it was just silly to address him so formally. "Constantine—"

He moved then, sprang to life like an unleashed jungle animal.

She gasped as he snatched her up and flung her back on the mattress as though she was weightless, a feather, a bit of fluff to be tossed and maneuvered for the pleasure of his big, unrestrained body.

He came over her, his nose deeply inhaling before descending and finding her throat, rubbing against her suddenly sensitized skin.

Heavens. He was . . . feral.

She should struggle. Protest.

Open her mouth and scream for help.

And yet as his nose buried in the crook of her neck, she turned her head and arched her throat, exposing more flesh for him. Offering him more. All. Everything.

Her gaze landed on one of his arms, braced taut and quivering beside her head. His nose and lips moved, grazing the line of her neck and she couldn't stop herself. She reached out and wrapped her fingers around his arm, curling her hand around his warm bicep, gasping at the singe of his flesh under her fingers, at the reciprocity of touch between them.

He jerked at the sensation of her hand on him, pulling his head back with a hiss and looking down at her with a mixture of astonishment and anguish. "No," he croaked.

"Constan—"

"No," he said louder, firmer. He shook his head once, twice, side to side. "No. Don't touch me. I can't if you . . . just put hands on me."

He flung himself away from her, landing on his back on the bed with a defeated groan. "You need to go. Now!"

She sat up and looked down at him, flipping her loose plait back over her shoulder. His long, lean body was sprawled amid the jumbled sheets like a splendid sacrificial offering. He flung his arm over his eyes as though needing to shield himself from the sight of her.

His manhood was still swollen, suffering and angry-red from neglect.

Enough of this.

"I *am* going to touch you." Ignoring his objections, she lifted her hand toward him. Until a thought seized her and she froze. "I don't repulse you, do I?" She bit her lip in consternation. She could not imagine touching him, subjecting him to her touch, if he found her repulsive. She could not bring herself to inflict that—*herself*—upon him.

His arm lifted from his eyes to stare at her in wonder. "God, no."

She exhaled. "Good." Her hand resumed its descent. She was almost to his abdomen. The skin there looked soft. Firm and soft.

Suddenly his hand shot out to seize her wrist. "Nora."

Her gaze locked on his, but it wasn't his hand that stopped her and held her in check. It was his intense gaze and the sudden doubt filling her.

He needed this like a starving man needed food, but he was unwilling. Not physically, but in every other way. Could she touch him knowing that?

Heavens. She hated that she had done this to him, that something she had created had done this to him—reduced him to this state. She felt wretched . . . as wretched as he looked twisting in agony upon the bed.

"I am sorry," she whispered. "This is all my fault."

"I asked for it." He nodded once in brave acceptance.

"But I knew what it could do to a person." She paused and shook her head. "I just didn't want to believe it could happen again."

His fingers around her wrist started to shake, as though his control was slipping, a rope unraveling from its mast. "I won't ruin you. You need to go."

"Is that what worries you?" She glanced back down to his manhood. It was still erect, pulsing before her very eyes, matching the swift beat of her pounding heart.

How long had he been like this? How long could he *continue* in this condition? It must be unbearable.

"What if you won't compromise me? What if I merely take care of your . . . er, situation?"

Merely? Nothing about this was merely.

Since Charlotte's marriage, Nora had seen fit to educate herself on matters of intimacy. She had always embraced knowledge on any subject, and she did not like knowing there was a gap in her range of knowledge, so she had researched to fill that chasm.

She had two married sisters and a houseful of females, especially since moving into Haverston Hall. Staff members gossiped and they didn't always pay attention to who was lurking about. Information abounded. She'd only needed to ferret it out.

Now, after much eavesdropping and snooping, she could say that she understood the basic mechanics of sexual congress. She even knew beyond basic mechanics. She knew there were ways to stimulate outside of traditional coupling.

She had learned there was more than one way to achieve release. Her sister had actually provided her with that gem of knowledge when explaining how the tonic had affected her. Nora was above all a scientist and demanded all details necessary to conduct her research.

"Come now," she coaxed. "Let me relieve your suffering."

His fingers loosened around her wrist and she knew he was relenting.

"What if I can't stop?" His voice came out

choked. "What if this tonic makes me . . . insistent. What if I become . . . rough?"

"I don't believe that will happen."

A pained grimace crossed his face. "What if I don't care . . . and take you like a beast regardless of your wishes?"

At his words, her skin broke out in gooseflesh. Her stomach gave a sharp twist that she felt all the way to her core. What was wrong with her? She fidgeted, pressing her thighs together and trying to ease the sudden throb. The suggestion of Sinclair taking her like a beast should not elicit a response and fill her with dark cravings.

"You won't. Not without my consent. I trust you. This tonic can't change your character. You're a decent man. No beast. You respect others too much."

His body jerked with another spasm. A fresh grimace passed over his face.

"Allow me." She pushed a little bit more, her voice dropping a pitch—sounding almost seductive. Except she knew she was not capable of such a thing. Seduction and flirtation were beyond her. Other people knew how to do those things. Not Nora.

Still, she persisted. She had to do this for him. "Let me help you." She scooted closer on her knees, looming over him. Releasing a determined breath, she instructed, "Now no more fussing and worrying. I am going to end your suffering."

Resolved, she nudged his hand aside and touched him. Closed her fingers around his throbbing shaft before the outrageousness of what she was doing chased away her resolve.

She was touching a man's member. His manhood. A . . . *cock*.

Yes, that was another word she had learned in her quest for knowledge. Just the sound of it in her head rang wicked and crude.

She was not touching just any man though. A man she had drugged with mind- and body-altering medicine. A man who affected her, who intrigued her on a cerebral level. And there was also the way he made her feel. Physically.

He made her *feel* physically.

That was new and profound.

She'd watched her sisters fall in love. She'd seen them blush and quiver when their husbands looked at them. Nora had thought it all stemmed from ridiculous sentiment, but now she knew sentiment had nothing to do with it. She was not in love with Constantine Sinclair.

But she wanted him. Her body quivered for him.

There could be lust with love. And lust without love. These two truths could coexist together.

That was a revelation. As was the way he felt

in her hand. Like silk on steel. Incredibly, it felt as though he was growing, thickening in her grip, and she had never felt so empowered in her life. She flexed her fingers around him and a hissing breath escaped from between his teeth.

She stilled, her gaze shooting to his face. "Am I hurting you?"

He shook his head, his dark hair falling across his forehead in charming disarray. He looked vulnerable, almost boyish—a marked contrast to the stern duke-to-be with never a hair out of place. Her heart squeezed at the sight. She longed to reach out and brush the strands away from his face. "Only when you stop. Please. Move your hand on me. Like this."

His hand came over hers, his long fingers wrapping around hers. He moved them together, his hand covering hers, sliding, rolling her palm and fingers up and down his silky length in a steady rhythm. He moaned and dropped his hand away from hers, letting her continue on her own.

She shifted and fidgeted, seeking the best position to appease her body's own burgeoning aches, especially the one between her legs. Nothing helped to achieve that, however.

"Are you still in pain?" she asked.

"The sweetest pain," he breathed, his eyes fluttering shut as though he were savoring her ministrations.

Nora settled down to recline on the bed, stretching out beside him, aligning her body to his and enjoying the contact, the brush of her breasts against his bare chest. She wished she were without her nightgown and robe, too, so that she might have the full experience of their skin rubbing together.

Truthfully, she was quite enjoying herself. The sensation of him in her hand was not at all what she had expected. She had thought to only bring him pleasure. She had not expected to find such pleasure in this act for herself.

She looked back and forth from his face to his splendid manhood. Both were beautiful sights. She rolled her thumb over the distended head of him. Moisture rose up to kiss her thumb and she rubbed the evidence of his desire over him, lubricating him.

More fluid rose and she used it to slick her hand over him, gliding faster over his stiff rod, her fingers exerting slightly more pressure and squeezing him harder.

He seemed to enjoy that. He growled and she watched his contorting face, riveted and hungry for every variation of his expression.

He pulsed, jumping under her touch and she gave him another squeeze.

"Bloody hell," he groaned, arching and thrusting in her grip.

The length of him, the generous girth of him folded in her hand, was as impressive as it was intimidating. Taking him into her body would be daunting.

Would be?

When had she started thinking of it as an eventuality?

She had vowed that would not happen but now, in this moment, she wasn't scared at the prospect. She envisioned herself mounting him and easing down on his member so that it filled the gnawing hollowness inside her.

Of course her thoughts had traveled there. It was the nature of sexual congress. How could she have her hand on his cock and not think about it? She eyed the length of him, wetting her lips. Her body was afire, the ache something fierce between her legs. She wanted this for herself. Not just for him.

"Nora," he said hoarsely, the sound a strangled plea.

Her gaze shot to his face again, ready to do anything right then—and not just because he was asking.

"Kiss me."

Anything but that.

Chapter 21

*N*ora stilled at his request. "I beg your pardon?"

She did not know why she acted as though she had misunderstood him. She had heard him perfectly well. Likely it was because the request struck such a deep chord of alarm in her.

She had never kissed a man.

Granted, she had never stroked a man's member before either, but the notion of kissing loomed as something much more personal and intimate and bound for failure. What if she was bad at it? She suspected there was skill involved with kissing.

She'd heard two maids tittering in the kitchens at home, giggling about the handsome and virile stablemaster's prowess as they simultaneously mourned the fact that he had fallen in love and married. Both lasses had agreed that Blackthorne was a good kisser whose lips would be heartily missed by all. If the stablemaster was a good kisser, then that meant bad kissers existed. What if she was one of them?

What if Nora was a bad kisser?

"Kiss me," he repeated, lifting his head up from the bed. "Nora. Please. Will you?"

Her gaze fastened back on his face. Gone was the composed duke's heir. There was no dignity in this man. This man pled for her lips, his face contorting and twisting with emotion as though he might die if he did not have them.

It's just the tonic. Not you.

"Nora," he said again. "Kiss me so that I don't feel as though I'm taking this from you. As though you are doing me a service with not a bit of enjoyment in it for yourself."

She jerked. Was that what he thought? That she was performing some regrettable chore?

Did he have no idea how she was affected? That she was consumed with the basest of desires? That she ached for him, too? That she suffered guilt for putting him in this dire situation?

"You take nothing from me. I did this to you, put you in this state—"

"Stop saying that. I volunteered. I knew the

risks." He lifted his head from the bed, the tendons of his neck stretched taut.

She could not take another moment of this. Seeing him in such torment, hearing him blame himself? She wanted only to end it. She wanted him to understand she was here of her free will. That she touched him with her free will.

She released his manhood and draped herself over him, stretching for his lips, determined to convince him this was no miserable chore for her. He needn't feel guilt on that score. If anyone should feel guilt, it should be her. She shouldn't enjoy this so much.

Her lips pressed clumsily on his without art or skill, but he did not leave it at that. He buried a hand in her hair, his fingers spearing through the thick mass, unraveling the loose plait she'd arranged for bed.

He tugged her closer and she obliged, clambering over him, her nightgown pooling over his naked form. She straddled him with her knees on either side of his hips.

It was shockingly freeing and delicious—the sensation of his big naked body under hers. Heat washed through her. She felt wonderfully afire, her breasts and womanhood aching for pressure.

One of his hands remained in her hair as he continued to kiss her, his tongue slipping inside her mouth. She opened her mouth wider so that their tongues could dance and tangle and rub sinuously.

"Nora," he moaned into her mouth. "My cock . . ."

She felt the rock-hard evidence of him, jutting through the layers of her nightgown and robe into her.

He moved under her, rocking, seeking his release.

He reached it at last.

Shuddering, he cried out, spilling himself as his hands dropped, clenching her hips, gathering fistfuls of the fabric in his fists. She felt the wetness on her nightgown as he stilled, his mouth open against hers, silent on a gasping cry.

She gasped, too, relieved he had reached his end—that it was over.

She was glad and relieved for him, but aching for herself. Bereft and empty. Unsatisfied. The fires he had stoked still burned within her.

She supposed that was her burden to bear.

She slid off him, releasing a pained breath. "Are you . . . improved?" She winced. Awkwardness was inevitable. There was no stopping it. How could they go back to the polite formality of before?

He tossed an arm over his brow with a gratified sigh. "I am . . . spent."

"No more . . . pain?"

"No."

She sat there, silent for some moments beside him, her fingers fiddling with the fabric of her night rail. "I don't suppose we should administer the tonic to Her Grace?" She released a shaky little laugh.

"No, you are quite right. Not without further testing. I had a spoonful. The next experiment should start with a droplet."

She nodded, looking up at the ceiling of his bedchamber and the flickering shadows and wondering when he thought that experimentation should occur . . . especially as she would be leaving tomorrow. That had not changed. More than ever, she felt compelled to put distance between herself and him.

Although the idea of departing prompted a pang in the center of her chest. She resisted the urge to rub her fingers there, to ease the ache.

"Indeed," she murmured. "Except I am departing tomorrow. Perhaps I can leave you with some of the tonic." Of course it was unlike her to leave an experimental tonic in the hands of someone else, but she felt an overwhelming urge to flee. The exception could be made this once.

He stared at her with a hooded gaze, his dark eyes unreadable.

A long moment passed and then he replied. "I cannot believe you scaled balconies to reach my room."

"What choice did I have? You would not open the door to me."

"I don't think you should leave on the morrow," he said suddenly, returning to the matter of her declared intent to leave, proving that he had in fact heard her.

Her chest tightened and she grew a little breathless. "Why is that?" She searched his face, longing . . . longing for *something*.

She was not sure what she hoped to see, but she recognized the emotion squeezing her chest. The hope that encircled her like an invisible band.

He nodded slowly, resolutely. "I'll not shirk my responsibility."

Her smile turned unsure, wobbly on her lips. She was not certain what he meant. What responsibility did he speak of? Curing the duchess? From the first moment she met him he had claimed that as his duty. She moistened her lips. "What do you mean? You've proven yourself to be a very responsible gentleman. Unfailingly so."

"I will do right by you."

Her smile slipped altogether, uneasiness sinking through her, the invisible band around her loosening as the hope faded away. "Right by *me*?" She shook her head. "I don't understand your meaning."

He waved a hand, encompassing himself and her. "I do not make it a habit to ruin well-heeled ladies."

Her stomach twisted and sank. Now she understood what he meant. He offered marriage. If one could call it an offer. It felt more like a stinging slap.

"I am not ruined," she said tightly between clenched teeth. Oh, how she despised that expression and all its antiquated implications. She lunged from the bed and glared down at him in his naked glory, trying not to let the sight of him thusly dazzle her.

"A gentleman does not dally with a lady and then *not* offer for her hand. It must be done. Honor demands it. You're under my protection whilst here and I abused that trust—"

She snorted. "Oh, spare me your noble altruism. I am not ruined like some bit of fruit that has gone sour and spoiled. I do not require saving. Any more than I require a husband."

His hands bobbed on the air as though attempting to mollify her. As though she were some wild steed in need of quieting. "Now, Nora. Be reasonable."

She sucked in a hissing breath. "Do not tell me to be reasonable. That's what men always say to women they cannot control."

His gaze widened and he looked her up and down appraisingly, his obsidian eyes staring at her as though he could see directly through her garments to the hollows and swells of her flesh beneath. "I would not be so foolish as to think you could ever be controlled, Nora."

Something stirred in her belly at his admiring look, at his deep voice and smoldering examination of her—a rekindling of the fire that had not yet been extinguished.

He tsked his tongue and continued, "Nor would I ever try to control you, Nora. That would be akin to sacrilege." His eyes swept over her again and it was tempting to forget that this man had insulted her with a backhanded proposal of matrimony.

And yet forget she would not.

She might not have been a girl with a head full of romantic dreams, but she knew how one ought to be proposed to and this was most assuredly not it.

She breathed in, fighting to reclaim her composure. "You had a problem tonight, sir, which I created, admittedly, so I corrected the situation for you. No harm done. You are not bound to me.

You need not give up the elegant Lady Elise and saddle yourself with the likes of me. That particular shame is not one you must endure." If her voice sounded cutting, she was glad for it. Let him feel every bit of her indignation.

"Nora. That is not . . ."

"Not the insult you intended?"

He stared at her in frustration. "That is—"

She continued, "Do not worry yourself. You're still free, fret not. Free to become the Duke of Birchwood without an unfortunate and embarrassing wife clinging to you."

She did not linger to hear the rest of his words. She had heard more than enough.

She marched a hard line toward the door. "If you do not mind, I shall use the door this time."

Without a glance behind her, she unlocked the door and exited his room, closing his bedchamber door with a clack, not even caring if a servant spotted her in the corridor.

Her reputation was not something she had ever overly valued. At least not her reputed virtue. At any rate, such a thing was a construct of men who wielded power. It was not anything substantial. Her reputation as a person, as a sister, as a friend . . . her reputation as a healer, those were the things she valued.

He did not know her at all if he thought she

would accept his insulting offer. Unlike most females her age, she wasn't after a husband. She was not trying to land a man. So many women needed their reputations as a bargaining device, a negotiating tool for security. Not Nora. She was privileged in that regard.

She realized she was fortunate to have a sister who had married well and would stand by her through anything. Yes, even a loss of reputation. Not that Nora believed herself without reputation.

She was still a maid. Her virtue was intact for all intents and purposes, and there would be no threat of tonight repeating itself. They were not lovers. This was a one-time liaison and he could stuff his sense of obligation toward her.

He'd only succumbed because of the tonic. He would not do so again.

He would return to his former self, the ever-rigid, ever-passionless and ever-proper heir to the Duke of Birchwood.

She took refuge in her chamber and undressed, glad for Bea's absence as she removed her soiled nightgown. She fetched a fresh one from her packed luggage, standing at the ready for tomorrow's departure.

She was no longer certain if she was leaving tomorrow. Her head ached when she contemplated it, so she decided not to give it another thought. At least for the remainder of this night. Tomorrow she would consider her fate. Tomorrow she would decide.

Once in a fresh nightgown, she moved before the washstand and poured water on the one she wore to Constantine's chamber. Taking the soap, she scrubbed it into the fabric, determined to rid herself of the evidence of their tryst.

Would that she could rid it from her mind as effectively.

Chapter 22

Constantine stood near the window in the duchess's bedchamber the following morning, observing the elderly lady where she sat in her bed, proppe up against several pillows. Thankfully, she looked in fine form, happily perusing the array of food on the tray before her.

"You know," Her Grace began, "the only thing that gave me any relief was that tea from our darling Nora." She sat cozily in her bed, lathering jam generously on her toast as though nothing unpleasant had ever afflicted her.

"Nora's tea?" The duke frowned. "Did not Sir Anthony help you?" The question was worded rather strongly, as though Sir Anthony *must* have helped her and nothing else. No one else. Certainly not Nora.

She waved a hand dismissively in the air. "Oh, nothing he does ever helps me. I don't know why you send for that man. There is nothing to be done for me when I'm in the throes of these spells, I fear, but Nora's willow bark tea is the closest thing to ever provide me with any relief."

The duke's frown intensified and he sent Constantine a rather uncomfortable glance, no doubt recalling how rude he had been to Nora.

Serves him right. Constantine felt a stab of satisfaction, hoping His Grace felt remorse for his treatment of her, and also inordinately proud that Nora alone had been able to provide even a modicum of relief for the duchess.

"I was desperate, m'dear," the man explained, taking his wife's hand in his. "I thought Sir Anthony—"

"Just because he attends your club and is a *man* does not mean he is proficient in medicine, my dear," she returned.

He puffed up his chest in a display of indignation. "I rather thought his medical license made him proficient in that regard, m'dear."

"Please." She laughed lightly and Constantine marveled that this lady was the same one to appear in such discomfort yesterday. "How old is Sir Anthony? Seventy? He received that license in the Dark Ages. I doubt he has kept up on any advances in medicine. Everyone knows he spends all his time with his mistress on Crawley Street."

"Maude!" the duke exclaimed.

Constantine laughed. He could not help himself.

"What? 'Tis common enough knowledge. Now please fetch Nora, would you? Even though I feel better, I would like some more of that tea of hers."

The duke looked to him questioningly. Clearly he expected Constantine to produce Nora as though she were naught but a servant to be managed. He certainly would make no such attempt after the abysmal way the duke had treated her . . . and perhaps Constantine was apprehensive to see her again after last night.

He did not precisely know how to comport himself after all that had transpired between them. He had tried to stay away from her. He had locked his door . . . and yet she had still found a way into his chamber, to him. It was difficult to accept that the tonic had broken him, but it had.

"Ah, I believe she is packing for home, Your Grace." He swallowed and fought to keep his expression neutral. At least that was what Nora had claimed the night before. She'd rejected his clumsy proposal. The fault was his. He should have done better. He owed her better. A gentleman did not offer marriage in such a blundering way.

"What?" the duchess exclaimed. "Oh, she can't leave yet. We've a dinner party tomorrow and I've invited my friend, Mrs. Prentiss, and her charming son specifically for our Nora."

Constantine looked at the lady sharply, his gut clenching for some reason. *Why specifically for Nora?*

"You cannot mean to entertain tomorrow night, my dear. You are not well—"

"Rubbish! I am quite recovered and just fine now."

"Maude, I forbid—"

It was the lady's turn to laugh now. "Oh, Victor, that is amusing. You've never forbidden me from anything. What makes you think you can start now and that I will listen?"

The duke opened and closed his mouth several times, clearly at a loss.

"Now." The duchess fixed her gaze on the maid standing nearby. "Please fetch Miss Langley, Polly, and inform her that I should like some of that splendid tea again. Quite restorative." She nodded brusquely and then turned to look at her husband. "I'll see the housekeeper now as well, to make sure all is in order for tomorrow evening. There is much to go over."

The duke's shoulders slumped. "Very well, m'dear."

NORA CAREFULLY CARRIED the tray of steaming willow bark tea to the duchess's bedchamber. The cook had (again) glared at her the entire time she had prepared it, clearly resenting Nora's presence in her domain.

Yesterday the glare had felt more *tolerant*, but it seemed the cook's tolerance for outsiders in her kitchen was waning. Today Nora felt the full, relentless blast of that glare. Apparently one day was to be tolerated, but a second day? Just barely.

Who knew what a third day of Nora invading her kitchen would bring? Fortunately, Nora would not have to find out Cook's reaction. She had reached her decision. Her things were packed and ready to go.

As soon as she delivered this tea to the duchess and visited for a spell, she would be on her way to the train station with Bea, and that much sooner to forgetting all about Constantine Sinclair and how she had briefly shared his world and did things with him—*to* him. Intimate and wondrous things that she did not imagine happening again.

Not with any other man. She would not feel the same craving for another man. It could not be duplicated. This much she knew.

She winced. It was all terribly complicated, compounded by his proposal. As lacking as she had found that proposal . . . there was a part of her that wished it had been real—that it had been different.

A footman held open the door for her and she entered the spacious bedchamber. The drapes were pulled back and the morning sunlight poured into the room.

The lady of the house was not alone. She had visitors.

Too late to turn back, Nora pressed on despite the room's additional occupants. Her gaze skimmed over the duke and Constantine and then looked away as she carried the tray to the bedside table and gently set it down. Even with her gaze averted, she felt Constantine's stare, sharp as a knife on her.

She did not glance to the gentlemen again as she addressed the duchess. "I'm happy to see you looking so well today, Your Grace."

"It just had to run its course." She nodded and looked pointedly in the direction of her husband. "That's what I keep telling him. I detest the bloodletting. I feel terrible afterward."

Nora followed her gaze to the duke, finally facing the sight of him. He looked at her with a hint of something in his eyes. Sheepishness, perhaps? He had, after all, spoken to her so horribly in his wife's bedchamber yesterday, prompting Sinclair to come to her defense. Birchwood had to feel a little awkward given the duchess had sent a maid to fetch her first thing this morning.

Nora tracked Constantine with her gaze. He stood near the window, bathed in the morning light. He looked no worse for wear from last night's events. At least there was that. He was well. No irreparable harm done.

He caught her looking at him and she snapped her attention back to the tea, pouring a cup for the duchess, mentally chiding herself when her hand unaccountably trembled.

"Here you go, Your Grace." Nora lifted the teacup up for the duchess with both hands, forcing them steady.

The lady accepted the cup and took a sip, wincing as she did so. "'Tis the most foul concoction, but it is effective at easing my muscles and aches and taking the edge off one's pain."

"Are you still suffering, Your Grace?" Nora asked, frowning.

The duchess slid a wary glance to her husband before answering, which informed Nora that there was indeed still some remaining discomfort, but she had no wish to openly divulge this truth. "No. Not really."

"Maude, m'dear." The duke tsked. "If you are still hurting you cannot think to entertain tomorrow evening."

"Oh, I have a few minor aches in my shoulders and my hips, which I live with most of the time," she snapped. "Rare is the day I do not suffer aches to some degree. I will not stop living my life and I most assuredly will not confine myself to a bed before I must do so."

Silence followed her outburst. The lady's hand shook ever so slightly as she lifted her cup and took a few more sips of the tea Nora had prepared for her. With a contented sigh, she handed the cup back to Nora.

"I'll leave your maid the recipe for the tea," Nora said, accepting the cup. "With instructions. As with any remedy, you could take too much. Don't exceed the recommended dosage." Papa had taught her to be moderate in the use of willow bark. Too much could be dangerous. As with anything . . . any tonic, the elements must be carefully balanced.

Heat crept up her face and she couldn't resist sneaking another look, only to find Constantine staring intently back at her. Of course. He was thinking of last night and how he had been affected from the dose he had taken.

"Well, I appreciate your thoughtfulness," the duchess interjected, "but you won't be leaving anytime soon."

Nora's gaze shot back to the lady reclining on the bed. "I was planning to leave today, Your Grace."

"Nonsense!" The duchess waved a hand in rejection of that notion. "You cannot leave today. Not when I've planned a dinner party tomorrow night with you in mind."

She blinked. "Me?"

"Why, yes, *you*. I've invited my dearest and oldest friend, Mrs. Prentiss, to dine with us. We've been friends ever since we came out together. She's a widow now, but she has the most charming son. Dotes on her, he does. Such a devoted lad." Her eyes grew misty and Nora suspected she was thinking of her own three sons, all lost to her. The moment passed, however, and she gave her head a slight shake as though clearing it. "You remember him, do you not, Constantine?" she asked in a voice that rang a fraction overly bright.

Nora followed her gaze to Constantine. He remained near the window, as upright and rigid as ever. "I believe so, yes. Always with his nose in a book."

"Ah, yes, that was true then and remains so today. My godson, Vernon, is quite the scholar." She preened, nodding as though that was the greatest endorsement she could offer to impress Nora.

"How . . . nice." Nora was not sure how to respond. "Literacy is always a good . . . thing." What else could she say?

"So no more talk of you leaving today. You must stay a little while longer." The duchess clapped her hands once and held them together as though that settled the matter. She waited then, watching Nora expectantly.

"I . . . um . . ." Her gaze drifted to the duke. After their exchange last night, she did not feel welcome here. He had made it clear he thought her inferior. She had been a harmless diversion in the duke's household until she went against him. She knew that now.

He stared back at her in silence, his lips pressed into an unforgiving line. He read her discomfort and he, of course, understood the reason for it. One word of encouragement from him would go a long way in appeasing her and making her feel welcome here again, and yet he held silent, locked in his aristocratic privilege. The man had likely never issued anything remotely resembling an apology in his life. He would not start now. She knew better than to expect that.

"I agree with the duchess. You must stay. I insist," Constantine spoke up, interrupting the staring spell between Nora and the Duke of Birchwood. "Her Grace has planned this dinner in your honor. You cannot disappoint her."

Nora considered him carefully, wondering if he was agreeing for himself or for the sake of the Duchess of Birchwood. Did he want her to remain for Her Grace? Or perhaps he wanted her to stay at Birchwood House, in small part, for himself?

It felt like a dangerous thought and something she should not even be wondering. There was no purpose in it. There was no hope or possibility of anything romantic between them. Last night had simply been a consequence of a difficult situation. The tonic was the reason behind their tryst and she needed to keep that at the front of her mind.

The duke frowned, the heavy lines of his face deepening. This time, however, his ire seemed focused on Sinclair. He did not even glance at Nora. It was as though she was invisible.

Sinclair looked back at the older man, his expression mild, unaffected.

"Indeed, Nora." The duchess nodded cheerfully and pressed the point. "You cannot disappoint me."

"Come now," Constantine coaxed. "You should have already left if you wished to catch the morning train."

A fair point. She had lingered in the duchess's chamber longer than she intended.

Constantine's lips twisted wryly and she wondered what he truly thought of her staying here longer. After she rejected his most insulting proposal last night—if one could even call it a proposal—she had assumed he was ready to see the last of her. No doubt even eager for it. Then he could get back to his life and courtship of the lovely Lady Elise.

Nora looked back and forth between them with a rueful smile. "How am I to deny such expert cajolers?"

"Brilliant." The duchess motioned to the tea that had undoubtedly gone cold on her bedside table. "We have much to do today in preparation."

"You should rest today so that you are in good form for tomorrow," the duke interjected.

"Hm," his wife replied noncommittally with a vague wave of her hand. "Where is Mrs. Blankenship? If I am to stay in this infernal bed, then I must see her to go over all the arrangements."

"Would you like me to locate her for you?" Nora offered.

"Oh, would you? Thank you, my dear."

Nora was only too happy to leave the chamber. Perhaps on her own, alone, away from them all, away from Sinclair, she could comprehend why she had agreed to stay here longer in this place where she did not belong.

Chapter 23

*C*onstantine waited a moment after Nora departed the room and then gave a mental curse. Excusing himself, he followed her as though an invisible string connected him to her.

"Nora," he called, attempting to catch up with her in the corridor.

She visibly stiffened, but continued walking as though she had not heard him. In fact, her strides seemed to quicken.

She intends to ignore me now?

Was this because of what they did in his bedchamber . . . or because of his colossal fumbling muddle of a marriage proposal? Perhaps it was both things. All the things. That seemed likely.

He had mismanaged every bloody bit of it.

His offer of marriage had *felt* the honorable thing to do at the time—but then he had not been thinking rationally. Not been *feeling* himself at all. He had been lost to the euphoric aftermath of his release.

Never had he experienced such a climax. It had to be the tonic. Certainly his reaction was not particular to Nora. Any female could have brought forth such a reaction. Certainly what he felt for Nora wasn't . . . unique.

She had simply relieved his . . . *affliction*. Because that was what she did as a healer. She cured people.

It just so happened to be that his affliction was a raging erection.

He had been hasty with his words.

Nora was still a maid. No one knew of her time in his bedchamber last night. Her reputation was intact.

He should never have offered for her. He'd been out of his head. Of course she did not want him for a husband. He had not known her for very long, but he knew already that Nora Langley was an unorthodox female. She was not after marriage. It was not something to which she aspired.

He lengthened his strides and called her name again.

Finally, she stopped. He stared at the back of her, noting the rigid set to her shoulders. Slowly, she turned, her reluctance evident.

She settled an icy cool gaze on him. "Yes?"

He exhaled. "Thank you. Thank you for staying. I know you wanted to leave today."

Her cheeks pinkened. "I did not do this for you. Let us be clear on that."

"Of course. You're doing it for the duchess."

She nodded slightly and some of the tension seemed to dissipate from her at his acknowledgment of this. "Her Grace has gone to the trouble of planning this dinner for me. I will attend."

"Of course." He nodded, not caring her reason for staying, only stupidly, unreasonably glad that she was.

She looked him over carefully. "How are you feeling this morning?"

Did she ask because she feared he was still afflicted with overwhelming lust and would pounce on her?

"I am fine."

"Did you sleep well?"

Better than well.

"Fine. Thank you."

He had fallen into a dead sleep after she left him last night, his body sated, happy and replete from her . . . assistance.

Even now, the taste of her lingered on his lips. He flexed his hands, his palms tingling as he recalled the shape of her hips in his hands.

It was a complicated thing. He was conflicted with wishing he had done more with her, *to* her, and regretting that they had shared any intimacy at all. It was all vastly inappropriate and vastly unfair to her. He knew that.

Without that tonic, without her invading his bedchamber when he was in such an unbridled state, he would never have touched her. He knew that, too.

Constantine would have continued to resist the allure of her because he was all about reserve and restraint and duty. And doing his duty by her meant keeping his hands, and most importantly, his cock, to himself.

He was courting another woman, on the verge of proposing to a female chosen for him by his family—the family to whom he owed everything.

He may be plagued with this troubling lust for Nora Langley, but he would not succumb to it. Not again.

The tonic may have broken down his will last night, but now he was in full possession of himself.

Today he owned himself entirely. There would be no further missteps. No more moments of weakness.

"I am glad to hear that. That is a relief." She nodded with a distracted air, her gaze averting his as though she could not tolerate the sight of him, and that stung. He did not want her uncomfortable or repelled by him . . . and yet that might be inevitable.

Footsteps sounded and they both turned to watch as a footman advanced down the corridor, his arms overflowing with fresh linens. He walked stiffly, eyeing them both.

Constantine took her elbow and pulled her to the side of the hall with him so that the man could pass.

The footman paused and nodded deferentially to Constantine. "Mr. Sinclair." The man then looked at Nora and his eyes visibly cooled as they rested on her. He inclined his head only a fraction, a scarce nod for her. It was apparently all the respect the servant could muster.

Anger stirred within him. He did not know why Birchwood's staff treated her so shabbily. It was not blatant. He could not call anyone out directly for disrespect. They did and said all the right and proper things, but it was there, a subtle rebuffing. It must stem from the duke.

The servants were always present. At least one of them, if not more, in every room at nearly all times. They had witnessed the duke's cold treatment of her and they took their cues from him.

The servant continued on his way.

Nora pulled her arm from his grasp. Her fingers went where he had held her, rubbing the exposed skin as though she wished to rid herself of his lingering touch.

That stung. Did his mere touch repulse her now?

Her gaze followed the retreating servant. "You need not hover about me so much," she said tightly. "Servants gossip. People talk."

He snorted. "I do not typically concern myself with what the servants think." Right now, he felt particular irritation for Birchwood's household staff.

"You should care," she snapped. "The servants hold a direct line to their masters. What the staff witnesses, what they know, what they *think*, does not stay private. Ultimately, it holds great weight."

He stared at her intently, assessing. She appeared truly concerned, her gaze fixed seriously on him.

"You don't strike me as someone who cares what others think," he murmured.

"I don't." She paused to inhale. "But you should."

"Me? Why should I care?"

She gave a brief laugh and took a careful step

away from him as though needing the distance. "You are going to be the next Duke of Birchwood. Appearances matter for you. That is your fate."

He wanted to deny that, but he could not. She was correct.

He would become a duke, and with that he would have all the responsibilities thereof, including the very stated expectation that he would take his cousin's betrothed to wife.

In that moment, he felt trapped, cornered. Was that the effect of dukedom? To make him feel like a caged animal?

Nora backed up several more steps. "We should keep our distance from each other for the remainder of my stay here."

He opened his mouth, wanting to deny that, to argue with that, but it made perfect sense. Of course. He should give her a wide berth. Given what had happened last night he should not even look at her, much less speak to her—and he should certainly never touch her, never be seen alone with her. That all seemed the most sensible course of action. It was not an unreasonable request.

He nodded to her as she retreated. "Very well."

She held his gaze for one lingering moment and then turned away.

He watched her go until she was out of sight.

"OH, THAT'S LOVELY," the duchess proclaimed the following morning, clapping her hands together as she admired Nora in her gown.

"You really did not have to do this." Nora grasped the luxurious fabric of her skirts.

"After how kind and attentive you've been to me? A new dress is the least I can do for you, darling."

Bea, crouched at Nora's feet, pinned the hem where it needed to be shortened. She nodded. "You look like a princess."

"Indeed," the duchess seconded, her eyes bright and lively. "You can wear this tonight. I am sure dear Vernon will be quite besotted at the sight of you. You look a vision."

Nora had lost count of how many mentions of Vernon had occurred this morning. Clearly, the duchess was matchmaking. Nora fixed a placid smile on her lips, her fingers continuing to work in the luxurious folds of her skirts.

"We need a ball gown for you, too, as I suspect there will be a magnificent ball in our future very soon."

The duchess waited, looking at Nora as though for great effect, to build anticipation. The lady glanced left and right, clearly fearing being overheard. Nora was not certain who she thought might eavesdrop as it was only Nora and Bea in the room.

The duchess dropped her voice to a whisper. "You could wear it to Constantine's betrothal ball."

Nora's heart yanked hard and locked, clenching to a full stop in her chest.

"Betrothal ball?" she echoed, her voice thin. "Is that set to take place then?"

Bea stilled where she crouched at Nora's feet as well. Her gaze lifted to fix on Nora's face, her eyes wide with what could only be characterized as keen interest.

If Nora had any doubt that Bea knew there was something between Nora and Constantine, something beyond simple friendliness, it was put to rest.

Bea knew. The woman was far too intuitive.

Bea perhaps knew what even she could scarcely admit to herself—that Nora held a *tendre* for Constantine.

She could not look at him without feeling butterflies in her stomach. Without her heart squeezing. Without her pulse racing and her mouth watering. Each time she closed her eyes she saw that beautiful body of his spread out before her on a bed and she physically ached.

Impossible. She could not have him. She gave herself a swift mental shake and schooled her features into impassivity. Bea could not know all of those things. Her maid did not know anything for a fact. She could have her suspicions, but that was all they were.

"Oh, it's not official yet," the duchess said. "But His Grace has spoken with Constantine. It is coming. There will be an announcement soon."

She nodded. *Good.* Hopefully it would happen very soon. The sooner the better. Truly.

The better for everyone.

Chapter 24

*S*he looked beautiful.

Constantine could not take his gaze off Nora over the dining table. She glowed like a jewel. Like flame. He could blame it on the gown. It was stunning and revealed Nora's most tempting shoulders and décolletage—her peaches and cream skin that was more peaches than cream. She was so sweet he ached for a taste.

Except the gown would not account for the way her eyes sparkled when she laughed at something Vernon bloody Prentiss said to her. *Vernon Prentiss.* She could do so much better than that sod.

Constantine's fingers clenched around the stem of his wineglass as she tossed back her head, arching that lovely throat. Candlelight caught in the lovely arrangement of her hair, gilding it like fire.

Prentiss could not be funny. Impossible. He had never been amsuing as a lad. He'd been a fussy sort, never one to play games or run about outside with the rest of the children. He also had a penchant for snitching on all their activities, right or wrong, to the headmaster. It had never been originated from any moral sense of justice either. He was merely about currying favor with those in authority.

Constantine did not trust Prentiss then and he did not trust him now. Especially not with the way he was looking at Nora.

The man drank deeply from his glass of wine as Nora talked. He licked the red from his fleshy lips, staring at Nora's much-displayed cleavage like that was the meal he preferred to be devouring.

Nora was moving her hands a great deal in that way she always did when she talked. It was particularly mesmerizing tonight—her flashing hands in front of the generous swells of her breasts.

He wished to grab her hands and hold them in place—or gouge Prentiss's eyes so he would cease to ogle her.

No. More than that.

He wanted to grab her and haul her from the

room. He longed to strip her gown off her body and bury his face in those breasts, to find and taste her nipples, to discover their look and texture, to watch her writhe under him as he buried his cock deep inside her sweet quim.

It was a wholly animal reaction. Perhaps the tonic had not dispelled entirely? Except he knew that to be only a weak excuse. He'd taken it long ago. It's power over him had long faded.

Her power over him, however, had not. He wondered if it ever would.

"Mr. Sinclair? Constantine?"

He tore his attention from Nora where she sat down the length of table. Lady Elise stared at him patiently, a kindly smile on her lips.

"Yes?"

"I was asking if you do not care for the fish?" She nodded to his untouched plate. He'd forgotten even placing the wedge of fish on his plate.

"I . . . no." He picked up his neglected fork. "I quite enjoy it." Then, unable to help himself, his gaze strayed to Nora again.

"Miss Langley looks lovely tonight, does she not?"

He snapped his gaze back to the woman to whom he should be devoting all his attention. "Ah. I had not noticed."

She laughed softly, almost inaudibly, and

reached for her glass with a shake of her head. Just before she brought the edge of her glass to her lips, he thought he heard her whisper.

Liar.

He looked at her sharply, studying her. He'd always judged Lady Elise to be intelligent, but he had not realized just how perceptive she was. She saw too much. Too much of him right now, at any rate.

He inhaled deeply and fixed a smile to his face. He needed to stop gawking at Nora and focus all his attention and energy on Lady Elise. She would make a fine wife. He had no doubt of that. She might have been intended for his cousin, and old Birchwood might be forcing her down his throat, but she truly was a lovely human being.

For the rest of dinner he managed to keep his attention where it should be. His gaze did not stray to Nora. Not even when he heard the lovely trill of her laughter.

After dinner, the men adjourned to the library for their brandy and whisky. Constantine managed to feign a relaxed air, staying put when Prentiss rose from his chair before anyone else. "If you'll beg my pardon. I think I will rejoin the ladies now."

The duke chuckled. "Ah, our fair Miss Langley has snared your admiration? It seems the duchess's matchmaking instincts are impeccable, as always."

"Of course Miss Langley is delightful and has her charms, but I would not go so far as to say that." Prentiss tugged at the cuffs of his sleeves, straightening his jacket.

"You will have to settle down some day, lad," the duke intoned. "Your mother will insist."

"Some day," he agreed and then offered a rather sly grin that Constantine felt the violent urge to wipe off his face. "But not anytime soon."

"Then what are *your* intentions with Miss Langley?" he asked, not giving a damn how aggressive the question sounded escaping him.

The man had just declared he was not interested in honorable marriage to any woman. So what did his flirtatious behavior with Nora mean then? Certainly he was not looking for any honorable liaison with Nora. Just a liaison then.

The duke chuckled. "You sound like an outraged papa, Constantine. Miss Langley is our guest here, but you needn't be so protective of her." His lips curled ever so slightly. "I think we can all agree that Miss Langley can take care of herself. She is a veritable bluestocking."

"So that means no one should have a concern for her well-being while under this roof?" he asked mildly despite his tumultuous feelings. He turned his glass around in his hand, his fingers rotating along the rim with deceptive idleness. "Is a *bluestocking* somehow worth less consideration?"

The duke sputtered, "N-no. That is not what I said at all."

Not what he said. But it was what he meant.

Ever since Constantine arrived here Birchwood had been schooling him on the things that, in his opinion, mattered. Things that were important to a future duke of the realm.

Nora Langley was not one of those things as far as Birchwood was concerned and he had made that abundantly clear.

Prentiss cleared his throat, looking confused. Perhaps justifiably. "I merely enjoy Miss Langley's company. She has quite a number of interesting theories, and she is a winsome lass. Who would not appreciate her company?"

"Indeed. On both accounts," Constantine agreed, still staring at the duke, finding him even more contemptible a person than Prentiss. It was troubling.

He'd always respected and admired the man, but now he was coming to the bitter fresh realization that Birchwood wasn't a benevolent man. His honor and generosity extended only so long as they did not infringe on the way he thought the world ought to exist.

Prentiss motioned to the door. "I'll . . . er . . . see you both in the drawing room shortly."

The duke nodded. "We will join you soon. Take Miss Langley for a stroll in the garden, why don't you? It's a fine evening. Spring is in the air."

The door shut behind Prentiss and they were left alone.

The duke and the heir.

They finished their drinks in silence. Words between them were unnecessary.

A line had been drawn. Tension throbbed on the air. They understood each other perfectly. Well, he understood the duke. Somehow he doubted that Birchwood understood him.

Men like Birchwood didn't understand those who weren't like him, and Constantine was beginning to realize that.

He was beginning to realize a great many things. One of which was that he could never be like the Duke of Birchwood. He didn't want to be. Those aspirations were quite finished.

Such a thing was an impossibility.

NORA TRIED TO pay attention to what Mr. Prentiss was saying.

It was a lovely evening for a stroll and he was

not her usual dinner companion. He was interesting and spoke on a variety of topics.

Like Nora, he was interested in botany. Aside of Papa, she had never met another gentleman who knew that without Carl Linnaeus the world would have no formal naming system for any living thing.

He'd returned to the drawing room ahead of Constantine and Birchwood. She wondered what was keeping the two gentlemen, and then she quickly told herself that she did not care. Constantine's actions were of no concern to her.

Constantine had sat at the other end of the dining table from her and every time she glanced his way he had seemed deep in conversation with Lady Elise. The sight had served as a proper reminder. They had no need for further interaction, and she had no business concerning herself with his actions.

"Miss Langley?"

"Hm?" She refocused on the gentleman beside her.

"Did you hear my question?" he pressed, his eyes gleaming at her in the evening gloom.

She supposed she had not. As interesting as she happened to find him, her thoughts drifted to Constantine again and again. Right or wrong, she could not stop herself.

She supposed he was in the drawing room by now. She did not imagine he would keep Lady Elise waiting for long. He was too gentlemanly for that.

Nora could see them now in her mind, their handsome heads bent close together in genial conversation.

"I'm sorry," she murmured. "Do you think we should return to the drawing room now?" She turned back in the direction they had come, to the well-lit house, not giving Mr. Prentiss a choice to the contrary. She had been somewhat coerced into the stroll. She was actually surprised at how readily the duchess approved their walk, beaming her assent when he asked Nora if she would care for a stroll.

She had obliged and now she was ready to return inside.

Mr. Prentiss stayed at her side, keeping a fast grip on her arm. She could not help noticing how his thumb moved in a small circle against the inside of her arm. She resisted the urge to yank her arm free and simply quickened her steps, eager to reach the room where she might be rid of his touch.

"So soon?" he inquired with an unbecoming pout to his voice.

Up ahead a footman stood sentry at the balcony

doors leading into the drawing room and a relieved breath slipped past her lips. "I should like to visit with the ladies, too," she responded vaguely.

"How long will you be staying in Town? There is a fine exhibit I should like to escort—"

"I will be departing at the week's end." She assumed so, at least. Perhaps sooner if she could extricate herself from the duchess. She had not chosen a particular day, but Nora could not stay here forever. She saw no point in remaining to attend Constantine's betrothal ball. Her presence was not necessary for that.

In fact, she preferred to be far away when that happened.

"Oh, well. There is some time then. Perhaps Wednesday you would like to accompany me?"

"I shall have to see what the duchess has in store for me. She keeps me quite occupied." Not an untruth precisely.

The footman opened the doors for them and they stepped inside.

She was correct in assuming Constantine would have joined them by now. She was also correct to assume he would be sitting beside Lady Elise.

"Ah! Back so soon," the duchess declared, sharing a conspiratorial wink with her friend, Mrs. Prentiss.

She looked to Constantine. He gazed at her with an unreadable expression.

"Ah. Yes." She nodded and lightly touched her temple, suddenly landing on the excuse. "I've a bit of an aching head."

"Oh. Hope you're not coming down with anything." The duchess tsked with a concerned shake of her head.

"Indeed. Perhaps you should retire early for the night?" the duke suggested, his expression as empty as ever when he looked at her. At least since she had dared to interfere with his and Sir Anthony's care of his wife and Sinclair had challenged him on her behalf.

Since that had happened, the duke's aversion for her was palpable even during this evening's dinner that the duchess claimed, ironically, was in Nora's honor.

"Yes." Clearly the duke desired to be rid of her, but Nora did not care. She clung greedily to the excuse, her gaze skimming Constantine with his elusive stare and Mr. Prentiss with his faintly hungry look. "I think I will retire for the night. Thank you for that suggestion, Your Grace." She would happily remove herself from this room and its inhabitants. "Good evening, all."

Turning, she departed the room, feeling a number of stares boring into her back.

CONSTANTINE STARED AFTER Nora even though it was evident she was gone from the room. He felt as though he were caught in some manner of spell—a trance—and he could not look away.

Conversation flowed around him in the drawing room, but he heard not a single word. He could not bring himself to focus on them. He continued to stare at the double doors as though she might return.

Of course she would not.

If he had the good fortune to leave, he would not return either.

"Mr. Sinclair?"

At the dulcet voice, he dragged his attention to Lady Elise. "Yes?"

She bestowed a forbearing smile on him. "Walk with me, would you, sir?" Without waiting for his answer, she rose and led the way outside in a gentle swish of skirts. Of course she was accustomed to being in command. Privilege granted one such a thing.

He followed.

Once outside, he offered her his arm and together they strolled through the gardens in companionable silence. He had never been so grateful for the fact that she wasn't a chatty female.

"Lovely evening," she murmured.

"Indeed."

Then, after some moments of peaceful quiet, she volunteered, "Miss Langley is a very accomplished young lady."

He slid her a cautious glance. "Yes. She is."

"Not very traditional."

"No indeed." He chuckled lightly. "She is not that."

"I don't imagine she would be interested in joining my sewing circle. We've been working on pillow lace the past two weeks."

"Ah," he said noncommittally, determined not to say anything to even indirectly insult Lady Elise's pastime. Although he could not help smiling. He could not envision Nora spending even an hour at such a task.

"Well, however disinclined to sewing she may be, I imagine she will one day be a fine partner to some fortunate gentleman."

Constantine stopped and faced her, no longer believing this was a casual conversation. Lady Elise's remarks felt very purposeful. "I imagine she will."

"You know, Mr. Sinclair, the world shall not cease to exist if you and I fail to make a match." She released his arm and moved to a nearby garden bench. Sinking down upon it, she lifted her face to look up at him expectantly. "Sometimes things simply aren't meant to be. Unions . . . are not meant to be. There are many unhappy *ton* marriages because people fail to recognize that."

He considered her. "I would agree with that assessment."

Although the world might cease to exist for the Duke and Duchess of Birchwood if he and Lady Elise failed to make a match.

Except Constantine found that he no longer cared. It appeared, based on the nature of this conversation, that Lady Elise did not care either. Apparently she was not overly attached to the notion of marrying him and he felt a great weight lift from his shoulders.

He could feel no sense of obligation toward her. He could go where his heart willed.

"Very good." Lady Elise nodded once. "I am so glad we have that settled between us. Now." She clapped her hands and pushed back to her feet. "Shall we return inside? I fear staying out here much longer only feeds their hopes."

"Indeed. Dally much longer and they shall have the wedding banns composed and ready for posting."

She giggled at his half-jest and took his proffered arm. "I suspect there could be wedding banns soon though. Only not for you and me."

He sent her a sharp look.

"Oh, come now." She arched an eyebrow. "Do

not look so very guarded, Mr. Sinclair. Give your-self time to sit with the notion and let it seep into you. You and Miss Langley would make quite the fine pair. As I said . . . some unions are not meant to be. Inversely, some are."

As he escorted Lady Elise back into the draw-ing room, her words echoed in his mind and he realized he did not need very much time to sit with the notion at all.

It had already seeped into him.

He already knew.

Chapter 25

Nora had just sent Bea off to bed for the night when a knock sounded on her door.

She'd permitted Bea to assist in the removal of her gown and brushing of her hair. Bea actually gave her little choice. She simply set to work on Nora, and Nora submitted. By now she had learned it would do little good to protest her maid's attentions. Bea would have her way. Nora might as well submit.

She moved to the door, breathing easier free of her corset and out of the gown the duchess had forced on her today.

It wasn't Bea. She never knocked.

It was likely the duchess or her maid, checking in on Nora.

Opening the door, she discovered how wrong she was. Neither the duchess nor one of her maids stood there.

It was Constantine, still wearing that darkly elusive expression.

He stepped inside, compelling her to take a step back. Closing the door behind them, he turned the lock with a soft *snip*.

"Wh-what are you doing in here?"

"How was your stroll with Prentiss?" He asked the question mildly enough, stated it evenly, without inflection, but there was still something in his voice that gave her pause.

She angled her head and eyed him, trying not to let the sight of him this close, alone in her bed-chamber, addle her thoughts.

"Lovely," she replied, noting that his expression darkened to a scowl. Did he not like Mr. Prentiss? "And how is Lady Elise?"

"Lovely," he echoed.

"Should you not be downstairs with her?"

"I'm right where I want to be."

With her? In her bedchamber?

Alone in this vastly inappropriate scenario?

It seemed uncharacteristic of him to place ei-ther one of their reputations at risk in such a way. He had much to lose. Lady Elise did not seem like a female to look the other way at her husband's (or husband-to-be's) indiscretions.

"How is your head?" His gaze flickered over her face as if seeking the answer in her features.

Her fingers moved to her temple. "M-my head?"

"It was aching. Remember?"

"O-oh." She shrugged, recalling the excuse she had used to flee the drawing room. "I'm fine."

"Good." He took another step closer. "I'd hate for you to be feeling poorly."

"That is . . . kind of you to say." She backed up a pace, inching deeper into the room.

"Nothing kind about it. Rather selfish of me, actually."

She frowned. "Selfish?"

"Indeed. If you were unwell then you wouldn't be up for this."

He advanced then, his body crowding her. The air grew charged, crackling between them.

She retreated, and he followed like a predator in steady pursuit. Her heart took flight like a wild bird in her chest.

All at once, she stopped. Excitement warred with wariness inside her. Lifting her chin, she froze in place, waiting.

He reached for her, tumbling her against him.

He wrapped an arm around her waist and lifted her easily.

She held her breath as he clasped her against him, suspended above the ground, her body pressed so tightly to his that it would be impossible to determine where either one of them ended and began. They were eye level and she found herself drowning in his dark gaze.

Then they were moving.

He was walking quickly with her in his arms, her toes dangling inches off the ground as he carried her.

She could scarcely digest what was happening.

Everything was sensation.

Was that her pounding heart? Or his? With their bodies plastered together, she could not know for certain.

He set her down carefully on the edge of the bed, and then he dropped at her feet, lowering himself before her until he was on his knees like some prostrated medieval knight.

She moistened her lips. "Wh-what are you—"

His hands landed on the tops of her knees, the heat of his palms singeing her through the fabric of her nightgown. "Let's rid you of this, hm?"

Before she knew what he was about, his fingers seized the hem of her nightgown and he yanked it up, over her knees, over her thighs, with rough and, to be honest, faintly thrilling movements.

She obliged, lifting her bottom so that he could continue pulling it up over her hips.

And that's how she knew she wanted this . . . how she knew she was totally and irrevocably lost.

Logic might have fled her, but her body knew what it wanted. Before her mind could recognize the truth, her body was already there. It knew. It was in total agreement with Constantine.

She wanted this.

She wanted *him*. She had since the night of the tonic. *No.* That was not true. She had wanted him before that. Certainly by the time he had taken her to Middlesex to observe the surgery. Because he knew she would *like* it. Because he cared for her pleasure.

He pulled the nightgown the rest of the way over her head and tossed it aside.

She sat naked, propped on the edge of her bed.

He came in closer, nudging her thighs open and wedging himself between them. He set his hands on her thighs and this time there was no barrier. No nightgown in the way, no interfering obstacle of fabric to bar him from her skin. Just his big searing palms gliding over the tops of her thighs.

She trembled, gooseflesh puckering her skin as he explored her body, skimming her flesh, touching and fondling her until she couldn't stop from moaning.

Sensation rippled over her. It was like her body didn't belong to her anymore. She shook and trembled, sharp little pants escaping her.

He moved from her thighs to her breasts. She jerked at the first contact. Her breasts felt heavy and alien in the cups of his palms. His head dipped, his tongue flicking over one nipple, then the next.

Her head dropped back on her shoulders, her hair swishing down her back as he sucked first one nipple and then moved to the other one, pulling it deep in the hot cavern of his mouth until she was shuddering and crying out, one of her hands flying to his head, diving through the thick strands of his hair, clutching him tightly to her.

His teeth toyed and worried her nipple, growling around it, "How I have longed to do this . . ."

She whimpered as his big hand palmed down her stomach.

She thrust out her chest as he continued sucking her breasts, gasping when his hand dipped between her thighs.

His dark hooded eyes looked up at her and he said thickly, "I think it's time to return the favor you bestowed on me."

"Oh," she whimpered, as much from that hot gaze on her as from the wicked, delicious things he was doing to her.

She quivered as he eased one finger inside her at the exact moment his thumb found and pressed down on a tiny little button of flesh at the top of her womanhood that she didn't even know existed, which was a shame.

She called herself a scientist!

How did she not know such a pleasure point existed on her own body?

She didn't have time to dwell on her foolishness. Too much was happening.

She fell back on the bed with a sharp cry, arms flung above her head in total surrender as her body leaped and convulsed.

Jagged little moans tripped from her lips, endless and unremitting as she broke, hot release washing over her. Spots danced before her eyes and then she was floating back down, her body easing.

But not for long. The calm was not to last.

His finger stroked inside her clenching channel, building the ache back to a boil.

She moaned.

"You feel so perfect," he growled. "So wet, so ready."

And she was. She heard the wet suction of his finger working in and out of her. She felt the moisture on the insides of her thighs. His finger slipped out to play in the moisture coating her sex. "Is this for me, Nora?"

"Yes." Her voice rose, broken and trembling.

His gaze fixed on her face as he lifted his finger and tasted it—tasted *her*, savoring *her* on him in a display of wicked, wanton pleasure. She didn't know this man . . . this side of him. She'd had no idea it existed.

A beast intent on devouring her. Every inch of her quivered in anticipation, in greedy hunger for more.

More of the beast.

"What do you want?" he demanded.

"*You.* I want you," she croaked. She wanted the beast in him to join with the one that prowled restlessly inside her.

Then he was gone. Moving. Unleashed as though he had been waiting for her permission.

She watched as he hopped up to his feet, gaping as he hastily and gracelessly shed his garments, tossing them aside and revealing the lean lines of his body.

He stood in front of her, as naked as she had seen him last night except he looked much more impressive standing over her in this moment. Bigger. There wasn't an inch of excess on him anywhere. Perhaps that was what years in the army had done for him, hardened his body so that it was a weapon to be wielded against the enemy.

Right now I want him to wield it against me.

The wicked thought couldn't be helped.

He was corded with sinew and muscle, skin smooth except for the narrow trail of dark hair that led to that *jutting* part of his anatomy she was already acquainted with.

Her mouth watered in memory.

Tonight she would feel that cock and not just in her hand. Her womanhood pulsed, aching with emptiness, craving to be filled.

He reached for her, his hands seizing her waist. He tossed her farther back on the bed and then came down over her, spreading her thighs wide to fit his body.

He braced each of his arms on either side of her as his face hovered over hers, tension rippling along his jaw.

His hips settled into the cradle of her body, his cock prodding at the core of her.

"Constantine," she begged at a whisper.

With a growl, he released himself. Pushed inside her with one slick thrust, filling her, stretching her deliciously.

"Ohh," she gasped at the unfamiliar burning sensation. "Wait a moment."

He stilled, obliging, but the pause cost him. She could see that, feel that in the strained look on his face, in the tightness lining his body.

She wiggled under him with a strangled sob, her fingers digging into his taut shoulders as if needing sudden leverage. "Oh, you feel so big inside me."

"You're made for me," he countered, his lips husking against her throat, biting down on her tender skin, sending a fresh rush of moisture between her legs.

"You feel that? You're ready for me."

Her hands slid down his back, finding and gripping his buttocks.

She felt her inner muscles flex and that astonished her. She could control that.

She clenched, deliberately tightening, reveling in his deep groan.

"Oh, you're milking my cock, Nora, please, tell me I can—"

She worked her hips, tilting her pelvis under him, taking him deeper with a small cry, desperate for pressure on the growing ache.

Her fingers dug into the tight swells of buttocks, urging him to—

With a growl of defeat, he pulled out and thrust then, driving into her. The friction sent sparks through her and she lifted her hips for him, greedy for more.

"You brilliant lass. You feel amazing."

Another thrust.

She arched, crying out, reveling in the thousand pinpricks of sensation bursting throughout her.

"Harder," she begged. Her hands tightened, reveling in how his buttocks flexed as he pumped over her, answering her plea, increasing his tempo and lifting one of her thighs, draping her leg around his waist and changing the angle of penetration, bringing himself deeper inside her.

She wept, tears rolling down her cheeks at the fullness of him sliding in and out of her. His mouth claimed hers, drinking in her cries. He kissed her senseless, his tongue sweeping against hers, arousing her on a new level, sending another rush of moisture to her sex where his cock worked in and out of her.

"How do you feel this good?"

Groaning, he continued thrusting between her trembling thighs, shoving her higher on the bed with each plunge inside her.

Her nails dug into him, hanging on for dear life.

A sob broke, twisting and turning into a keening cry. His hand came over her mouth, muffling the sound.

It was astonishing. She didn't know it could be like this. She didn't know her body could feel these things, that her heart . . .

"Go ahead. Scream into my hand," he encouraged.

She writhed under him, her body out of control, without grace or rhythm now.

He drove into her again and she broke, exploding in a violent burst. Her tears streamed down her cheeks. "Constantine," she cried into his palm and went limp, quivering in the aftermath.

He didn't stop though.

He continued riding her, pumping relentlessly.

His hands clenched around her hips, hauling her in for his plunging cock. "Almost there," he panted.

She gasped, feeling the slow stir again, the build of sensation. "Oh, oh, oh."

He was unrelenting, driving into her ruthlessly.

"I can't . . . not again." Her head rolled side to side on the bed.

His thrusts came faster, harder, pushing her again to the edge of release.

She clutched at him, her hands clawing, moving up his back. He launched her over the edge again. Unbelievably. Incredibly.

He plowed her body like a man, no, a beast, released from his cage after years of captivity, all savage intensity. As though his life depended on reaching his climax.

A few more strokes and he stilled, arching his throat and tossing back his head with a groan as he broke and spilled inside her.

Her breasts rose and fell in heavy pants.

He lowered his gaze back down to her and she knew she looked astonished, ravaged.

Wrecked.

Because that was how she felt.

She couldn't steady her breathing. Not yet. She pushed back loose tendrils of hair from her face and stared up at him, fighting to regain her breath. "Oh . . . my."

"Oh my, indeed." He rolled off her and fell on his back beside her, flinging his arm over his face.

She turned her face to the side to study him, taking comfort in the fact that he was breathless, too. She supposed that meant he felt as shattered as she did.

She smiled, resisting the urge to reach out and touch him. That felt . . . *clingy.* Like someone who needed emotional reassurance following physical intimacy. That wasn't her. She frowned, an uneasy feeling settling in the pit of her stomach.

It couldn't be her.

Silence descended. She held still, wondering, waiting as the seconds ticked. How long would they stay like this? How long would he remain here? In her room? In her bed?

It couldn't be much longer. They didn't have that luxury.

"Well," he pronounced, lifting his arm from his face. "It is clear what must be done now."

Chapter 26

$\mathcal{N}$ora took a moment, rolling his words around in her mind, turning them over curiously . . . those words that he uttered rather grimly. *What could that mean?*

She moistened her lips. "What do you mean?"

"It is clear what must be done," Constantine repeated with a touch of insistence. "What we must do."

She reached for the counterpane and pulled it over herself. Serious conversations probably functioned better if one wasn't naked.

He frowned as she covered up her nudity, as though he preferred she remained naked.

Perhaps he did not agree with her logic, but she felt more composed at least.

"I'm afraid I fail to understand you." She shook her head in confusion. "What is clear?"

"After what just happened? Is it not obvious to you?"

Several things were obvious to her as she clutched the counterpane to her bare breasts. The primary item being that she was entirely too enamored of Constantine, which was insupportable.

She had thought she could do this. She had thought a physical liaison, a tryst, was possible without engaging one's heart. She thought she was a sensible female who could balance such a thing.

And perhaps it was possible.

Only not for her.

Apparently, Nora was not capable of an affair. Or at least she was not capable of a meaningless affair with Constantine. Apparently, she was equipped only for something *meaningful* with him and that, unfortunately, wasn't to be.

She tightened her grip on the counterpane and sat up, glancing from him to the door.

When was he leaving? Would he not take himself from her bed now? Her bedchamber? Is that not how these things, these trysts, were done?

He continued, "After this"—he motioned between them—"we haven't any other choice."

They would speak candidly of this then? She had not been convinced they would.

Constantine was not a man of excessive words. Nor was he the manner of man to proclaim his feelings or easily own his emotions. She wasn't sure he possessed any softer sentiments at all.

Just an inflated sense of honor and duty.

She was duty to him. Nothing more. And that truth stung. Again, proof that she should leave this house as quickly as possible and take herself home where she knew every bump and ridge in the terrain, where nothing could surprise . . . or hurt her.

At any rate, what could he say?

However shattering, this had simply been a physical act. It was no more complicated than that. At least it would not become complicated. She refused to allow it to become a difficult thing. Especially considering she would be leaving.

He stared at her steadily, his impatience palpable, crackling on the air between them.

"I must confess, what you speak of is not obvious to me."

A flash of exasperation crossed his face. "Come now. You're clever. I don't see how you haven't reached the same conclusion I have."

"I'm sorry. I must be obtuse," she snapped, glancing at her bedchamber door again, wishing he would simply leave.

He motioned between them again. "We cannot pretend nothing happened between us."

"Very true, we cannot do that. But we can make certain it never happens again."

"That is neither here nor there. Whether it happens again or not, the damage has been done."

Damage? She flinched. *So what happened between them was damage?*

She may have decided they would not repeat tonight and she would remove herself from here, but she had not thought of it in those harsh terms.

Her gaze slid toward the door, strategizing how she might get him to leave without just telling him to leave.

She faced him again. He looked at her expectantly, arching one eyebrow.

"Yes?"

"Need I be the one to say it?"

Her chin lifted. "I think you're going to have to."

"You are irreparably compromised."

She blinked. At least he had not said *ruined* again. She might have slapped him if he had.

He held up both hands and pumped them in the air as though encouraging her to say something, to reach what clearly, to him, seemed an obvious conclusion.

"I'll speak to the duke tomorrow and then we can travel to Brambledon to—"

"Wait. What? Why would you want to travel to Brambledon with me?"

"To inform your family that we must marry. Of course."

Of course.

Must marry . . .

The word *must* made her feel faintly sick. She pressed a hand to her suddenly roiling stomach, wishing she could scrub the sound of it from her ears.

She laughed mirthlessly. "You really know how to charm a lady." She held up two fingers. "I've been insulted with two thoughtless proposals from you now. *Two.*" She angled her head. "But can we even call these proposals since you have *proposed* nothing? You simply told me what we're going to do as though you hold authority over me."

"Nora," he began.

"I took you into my body. I did not give you leave to take over my life."

He flinched and it was most satisfying. Wrong or right, it felt good to see him affected . . . maybe even hurt.

Because she was hurting. She was hurting so deeply.

"I'm sorry. I did not realize there was any other conclusion to be drawn after—"

"Get out," she demanded, looking away from him, unable to look at his face, wondering at the pain sweeping through her.

She should not feel like this. Not at all.

"Nora, we have to talk about this and do the correct thing here. The responsible thing."

There had been nothing correct or responsible about what just occurred in this bed. It had been desire. Lust. How could he not see that?

It had been emotion.

Rare emotion from him . . . *and* even from her.

It had been love. Apparently he did not realize that or feel the same way.

She loved him. Foolishly, she had fallen. Just as her sisters had. She was not immune, after all.

She forced her gaze back on his face, blinking back the burn of tears. "I'll not suffer a third *proposal* from you. Go. Leave." She uttered the word *proposal* as though it were the foulest of epithets.

He stared back at her and she knew he was contemplating his next move. She didn't look away. She fixed her hard stare on him, letting him know she was serious.

He stood and donned his clothes. Dressed, his jacket in his hands, he faced her. "We'll talk tomorrow." Turning, he left her chamber.

They would not talk tomorrow.

Tomorrow she would be gone.

Chapter 27

*I*t felt oddly familiar as Nora and Bea crept from the house before anyone was awake.

Bea had not liked being roused from bed so early. She had plenty of questions. None of which Nora answered. She certainly was not going to share her motivation for their sudden and surreptitious departure. It was her private business. Not Bea, not anyone, was entitled to know that she had surrendered her heart to a man who did not want it. Broken hearts were a secret matter.

Dawn was splitting the sky as they arrived at the station. A porter helped them with their luggage, carrying it inside the mostly empty building.

"It's so early. There won't be a train for hours,"

Bea complained as they approached the ticket stand.

Nora ignored her and fished the money out of her reticule to pay their fare.

Bea continued, "Why did we have to arrive here so early? We could have enjoyed breakfast first."

"Because I did not want to encounter anyone in the duke's household."

"Are we running away then?" Bea's frown deepened. "What happened? What did you do?"

Nora shook her head swiftly, bristling at Bea's very accurate assumption that something had transpired. "Nothing," she lied. "I have done nothing."

Except fall in love with a man who was all about duty. A man who was so far removed from her that marriage to her would be viewed as his greatest failure by his family and peers alike.

Tickets in hand, they found a bench to sit on and waited for the arrival of their train.

SHE WAS GONE.

Nora was gone.

Constantine had scarcely slept a wink since last night, tossing and turning, and playing over how badly he had botched everything with Nora. What was wrong with him? Why couldn't he find the right words with her?

He rose from bed this morning with the resolve to make everything right. To win her. He had to win her and it had nothing to do with duty. It had nothing to do with obligation or the fact that he had compromised her last night.

He wanted her. He wanted her for his wife. In the clear light of dawn, he recognized that. He may not deserve her, but he wanted her.

Dressed, he departed his chamber with eager steps.

He wanted her for her.

He would begin by telling her that. That was his plan. Except she was gone.

She and her maid and all of their belongings were gone.

She had to have left very early this morning as no servant had seen them depart. As far as he knew, she didn't know anybody in Town.

She had to be leaving for home, returning to Brambledon.

That meant she had gone to the train station. Hopefully, she was still there, waiting on a train. If he hurried, he could stop her. He moved for the stairs at a run, skipping steps as he descended.

"Constantine," the duke called out to him, spotting him as he passed quickly through the foyer.

"Sorry," he called out with a distracted wave, not even slowing his pace. "No time to talk. Bit of a rush."

"Ho! Hold there!" The duke wasn't to be deterred. He moved faster than Constantine had ever observed, cutting in front of him and blocking him from passing through the front door. "Where are you off to in such haste?"

Constantine exhaled with exasperation, disinclined to reveal his purpose to the man. For one thing, it would require time he did not wish to waste.

"I will return soon and we can talk then, Your Grace."

He sidestepped around the man in his anxiousness, stopping abruptly, however, at the duke's next words. "You're going after the Langley chit."

It was not a question. It was a statement. Birchwood knew. He knew she was gone.

Constantine turned slowly to face the old man. "How do you know that?"

Birchwood shrugged. "I was standing at my bedchamber window early this morning. I saw her and her maid sneak off like two thieves in the night with their luggage." He sniffed in disapproval.

Constantine took a hard step toward him and then stopped, his hands curling into fists at his sides. "You didn't try to stop her?"

"Why would I do that?"

Constantine stared at the man for a long moment, letting that question take route before he finally answered with a truth that was not difficult for him to acknowledge. "Because I'm in love with her."

He scoffed. "What does that matter?"

"It matters because I want to marry her."

The duke laughed harshly then. "You've always been soft. Just like that father of yours, marrying a woman so beneath his station."

"Careful," Constantine warned.

Birchwood continued as though he had not spoken. "She was Greek, you know. Your mother's family. Your grandmother did not even speak the Queen's English." He shook his head in disdain. "Your father was a fool."

Constantine glared at him, seeing the man more clearly than he ever had. For months now, the man had been schooling him, training him, showing him how to be a duke, showing him the way in all matters . . . showing him how to be *like* him.

The man continued, "Do you think you love the chit? Fine. Shag her. Put her up as your mistress. You don't marry a girl like that."

"I will marry her, if she will have me."

"Don't be a fool like your father."

Constantine motioned to the door. "I'm going after her. I'll return later for my things."

"Your things?" The duke shook his head in bewilderment. "I don't—"

"That's correct. I've learned all I want to learn from you and I'll be moving into a house of my own."

"Now see here, Sinclair!" His face reddened. Blustering, he stabbed a finger after him. "You cannot think you can simply inherit my title and fortune and know how to properly manage—"

"Oh, I can and I will inherit your title and fortune because that is the law." He turned on his heels and opened the front door. He looked over his shoulder. "And I will manage just fine."

"IT'S TIME TO go," Nora announced as their train was called for the second time.

She and Bea had obtained a porter to help them with their luggage and they maneuvered through the station, much more crowded now than when they had arrived. Voices buzzed around them and train whistles blew alongside the rumble of steam engines.

Bodies bustled into them, and someone bumped into Nora. She dropped her reticule and bent to pick it up. Straightening, she paused as a single shout split the air, amid all the other noises.

"Nora! Noraaaa!"

"Is someone calling you?" Bea looked from her to the area around them, scanning the many faces.

Trepidation tripped down her spine, heightening her sense of urgency. "Of course not. Come. Let's go. We don't want to miss our train." She tugged on Bea's arm and hastened forward.

"Nora!"

Bea pulled back on her hand. "Oh, come now. Did you not hear that? It was definitely your name."

Bea looked back into the crowd, and Nora reluctantly followed her gaze.

"There!" Bea stabbed a finger in the air.

Stomach plummeting to her feet, Nora froze, watching as Constantine darted through people, bumping into them roughly with little regard to courtesy.

Bea looked back at her with a smug look. "What's he doing here, I wonder?"

She shrugged, shaking off her astonishment at seeing him there. "I don't have any earthly notion. Perhaps he has come to collect someone."

"Indeed. *You.*"

She shot Bea a glare. "We are going to miss our train." Almost on cue, the final call for their train bellowed across the air. Bea didn't budge. "Fine," Nora snapped, a fiery ball of desperation spreading through her chest. "Stay here or join me. I'm going."

She turned stiffly. With a nod for the porter, she continued on her way.

Of course, she did not make it very far.

A hand clamped on her arm and spun her around. "Nora!"

"What are you doing?" she hissed, glancing around them. It's not as though they had any privacy for this encounter. This was a very public place.

"Why did you leave?"

"We've said all there is to say."

"I haven't said all there is to say." He beat his chest with his palm for emphasis. "I have a great deal more to say to you."

She laughed humorlessly. "Oh, no. You have said *more* than enough. Please, say nothing more and let me go with as little spectacle as possible. I know you don't want that."

She snorted. Indeed not. The Duke of Birchwood would not appreciate that. It could generate rumors about his precious heir.

"I could give a bloody damn about spectacles," he growled.

She jerked at his voice, loud enough for the people around them to hear. She glanced around them. Several people stopped to gape at them.

"You don't want to do this," she warned. "Lady Elise could—"

"I don't *care* about Lady Elise. I care about you!"

"I knew it!" Bea declared nearby from gawking distance, grinning madly. She nudged the porter as though he were privy to the situation.

"Are you . . ." Nora glanced around and then added in hushed tones, "Inebriated?"

He blinked. "What? No! I am completely of sound mind. I am perhaps the most clear-headed I've ever been!"

Nora frowned, squeezing the bridge of her nose. "What's come over you?" She shook her head. "This is not like you. You're not . . ." *An exhibitionist. Emotional.*

"What's come over me?" He laughed and the sound was almost giddy. "You!" He spread his arms wide. "You have come over me."

People were definitely staring now.

"Hush." Nora waved at her lips as if that were indication enough he should silence and put a stop to his very public display.

"I'm sorry I offended you before . . . I won't do so again." A determined glint entered his eyes.

"What are—"

She did not get the rest of her words out. He dropped before her on his knees and seized her hand.

Bea squealed from nearby. People surrounding them gasped. A crowd seemed to grow. She even heard the hiss of his name. *Sinclair.* Soon followed by *Birchwood.*

Of course he was recognized.

"Nora . . ." He took a breath and lowered his voice. Suddenly, in this moment, it was just the two of them. "Will you marry me?" His third proposal . . . but this time done the right way.

She shook her head. "Constantine, you don't want to—"

"I *want* to marry you."

She looked down at him, fighting hard *not* to enjoy the warm clasp of his hand around hers too much. "Why?" she demanded. "You want to marry me? Why?"

A pregnant pause followed her question.

Everyone around them seemed to be waiting, too. Holding their breaths in collective silence.

He smiled slowly and she felt the warmth of that grin spreading like sunlight through her. "Because I love you."

That warmth exploded into fire in her chest. "You don't."

"I do."

He pushed to his feet and seized her face in both of his hands. "I love you. I love you and I don't want a future with anyone but you."

"But . . . you're going to be a duke—"

"I am foremost a man. A man that can be whatever kind of duke he wants to be . . . as long as I have you with me. As long as I have you at my side. I want to be happy, Nora, and I can't be that without you. Please. Make me happy. Let me make *you* happy."

"Constantine," she whispered.

"Nora," he returned. "Say, yes. Say you love me—"

"I do love you—"

"Then that's all that matters. Say you'll marry me and together we will build a life. One that we both want. You and me." His pressed his mouth to hers, right there in the middle of the station, in front of everyone.

She heard a garbled shout of encouragement from Bea, but she could not process the words . . . and she did not care.

All her attention was fixed on Constantine. "Yes. I'll marry you." He kissed her then, again, to shouts and applause and the roar of a train engine, taking its departure without her.

He lifted his head, his eyes gleaming brightly down at her. "You missed your train."

She smiled back at him. "I didn't miss anything."

Epilogue

Ten years later . . .

After donning and casting aside no less than five garments, Nora settled on a brown and cream striped day dress with a minimum amount of bustle.

"You are certain this is the one?" Bea asked, gathering up the discarded dresses.

Nora examined herself critically in the mirror, turning to observe herself from every angle. "Yes." She nodded with satisfaction. "This is the one."

The day dress was modest and functional. She should be able to maneuver about in it with ease, and the jaunty little lace at the collar was smart and struck her as quite studious.

"It is rather . . . plain," Bea offered with a wrinkling of her nose.

"Plain is not a bad thing, Bea. I am not going to a garden party."

"Hm." Bea sniffed and Nora knew her thoughts perfectly. As far as her dear maid was concerned, Nora should always be attired as though she were going before the queen.

Nora, however, did not wish to proclaim to the world that she was a member of the aristocracy—even if she was. The goal was to look presentable and not stand out as anything other than a first year medical student.

Sometimes she even forgot that she had married an heir to a dukedom. She rather suspected that her husband forgot, too. Or at least that he did not care. He preferred to live as Constantine Sinclair and not the Birchwood heir.

One day, in the future, the title would be his. When that day arrived, he would accept it—*they* would accept it. On their terms. Together.

He would define the role and not the other way around.

Naturally, Nora and Constantine did not fill their days with balls and routs and social calls.

They did not visit court or pander to the Duke and Duchess of Birchwood. They lived their own life together and it was splendid.

They had seen very little of the Duke and Duchess of Birchwood since they had married. They'd chosen a different path and it was not one the Duke of Birchwood approved, but Constantine did not mourn the loss of the duke's approval. Indeed not. They spent much of their time contentedly at home in the country. They had only just recently moved back to Town in time for Nora to begin medical school.

Up until this point, Nora had continued practicing the herbal arts and medicine whilst Constantine had turned his energy to matters of veteran affairs. There was very little in place for soldiers upon returning home, so Constantine had created multiple charity houses to support injured and aging soldiers, helping them acclimate and ease back into society. They each had their separate vocations as well as each other—as well as their life together.

And it was a wonderful existence.

"Well, if plain is your goal, you have succeeded," Bea declared.

Nora rolled her eyes. "Thank you, Bea. As always, your honesty is valued."

"Quite so." Bea nodded efficiently and stood back with a proud smile. "Now. Good luck today. You've worked hard and you deserve this."

Nora stepped forward to embrace the maid she had so long ago insisted she did not want in her life. So very many things had changed since then. She never thought she wanted a husband. She never thought she wanted children. How very wrong she had been on all those counts . . . and how happy she was in her wrongness today.

After inspecting herself one final time in the mirror, Nora nodded at her reflection. She felt suitably attired and ready for her first day. Not only *her* first day, but the first day for *all* female medical students in Great Britain. It was a momentous occasion. Historic even.

She would be entering the London School of Medicine for Women as one of its first students since the passing of the new medical act allowing the licensing of all qualified persons to be doctors, regardless of gender.

She descended the stairs with a flurry of butterflies spinning through her stomach. She entered the dining room to find it already occupied. Her husband sat with their four-year-old daughter on his lap. They ate from a bowl of fruit. Little Theodora took turns feeding herself and then her father with her usual air of confidence.

"Mama!" Theodora cried merrily, waving a half-eaten strawberry in the air.

"Oh, Con," Nora chided. "Her face is a mess."

Nora rounded the table and picked up a napkin to wipe her young daughter's juice-stained face. Satisfied she had wiped it as clean as possible, she bent down to press a kiss on her daughter's berry-scented cheek. "Good morning, poppet." Then, she turned to her husband, accepting his proffered kiss.

"You are looking very fine today, Nora." His eyes twinkled with amusement and she knew he knew how much she had agonized over her choice of attire. "How are you feeling this morning?" He stared closely at her face. "Excited?"

"Mostly nervous," she said as she lowered herself into the chair beside him and Theodora. "Only in the best way though."

"I am certain you shall astound them with your knowledge and wit."

She served herself some tea and toast. Her stomach might be a riot of butterflies, but she needed sustenance to get her through this day. "Oh, I don't know about that. All the other students will be very clever, too." Reaching for the jam, she began to generously lather it on her bread.

"But how many have your experience? Your practical skills shall mark you as a natural at once."

"You are only making me more nervous in saying that." She crunched down on her toast and chewed a little anxiously.

Con sent her an affectionate wink and readjusted their daughter on his lap so that he could reach across the table and give her hand a small comforting squeeze. "Just think of that brazen creature who forged her name and dispensed medical advice to all and sundry because she did not question her competence. That woman had faith in her expertise."

She laughed lightly. "Amazing how that was once a black mark against me and now you praise me for it."

"I was an ass then. Now I know better." He shrugged lightly. "It took me some time to understand that you're as brilliant as you are beautiful."

Theodora chose that moment to parrot her father. "Ass, ass, ass, ass, ass."

Nora laughed harder, shaking her head. "See what you've done now."

Constantine shrugged unworriedly and pressed a kiss to Theodora's cheek. "She'll soon forget it."

"If you say so." Nora snorted dubiously and lathered a fresh slice of toast with jam, extending it to Theodora. The child grasped the toast and greedily bit into it, filling her mouth with something other than expletives.

"Mmm," Theodora moaned in approval.

The clock tolled the hour and Nora rose hastily. "Goodness! I need to go."

Constantine pushed up from the table. "Let us escort you out."

The three of them departed the dining room. Theodora latched onto Nora's hand. In the entry hall, Nora squatted to embrace her daughter, inhaling deeply her sweet little girl scent that was now mixed with the aroma of tart blackberries. "Be a good girl today. I will see you at dinner, my love."

When it did not appear that Theodora would let go of Nora, Constantine stepped in and relieved Nora of their daughter. "Let's clean up and get ready for the park, poppet."

Theodora clapped her chubby hands at the prospect of the park. She loved her outings.

With their daughter in his arms, Constantine bent down and pressed a lingering kiss to Nora's lips. "Enjoy your day. Play nicely. Make friends. Learn." He pressed another quick kiss to her mouth. "And remember. We will be here for you when you get home."

Author's Note

If you're curious about the Duchess of Birchwood's mysterious malady, allow me to enlighten you. Not very long ago a member of my family was diagnosed with an inflammatory disorder called polymyalgia. Incidentally, when I mentioned this in conversation to a friend, I learned that her own mother was also plagued by the same ailment. I had never even heard of this condition, but suddenly I was thinking about it a lot and considering what a challenge it must be for those afflicted.

I don't profess to be an expert, but (as related to me) the muscle pain can be quite excruciating and most commonly afflicts women over the age of sixty.

Unfortunately, this condition was not identified in the Victorian era. As there is no cure for polymyalgia, and treatment is very limited, there would not have been much relief available in the nineteenth century to help our Duchess of Birchwood . . . but fiction is a wonderful thing. Anything can happen in books and I like to think that Nora not only perfected and fine-tuned her tonic to the benefit of the Duchess of Birchwood, but for all her future patients.

After all, I only write happily-ever-afters.

Of course that is what happened.

At Avon Books, we know your passion for romance—once you finish one of our novels, you find yourself wanting more.

May we tempt you with . . .

- **Excerpts** from our upcoming releases.
- Entertaining **extras**, including authors' personal photo albums and book lists.
- Behind-the-scenes **scoop** on your favorite characters and series.
- **Sweepstakes** for the chance to win free books, romantic getaways, and other fun prizes.
- Writing **tips** from our authors and editors.
- **Blog** with our authors and find out why they love to write romance.
- **Exclusive content** that's not contained within the pages of our novels.

Join us at
www.avonbooks.com

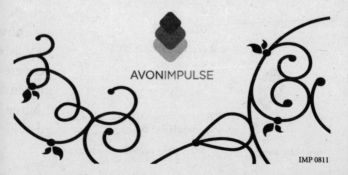